Secrets and Truths

Whitney Hill

BENU MEDIA

SECRETS AND TRUTHS
Copyright © 2022 by Whitney Hill

Benu Media
6409 Fayetteville Rd
Ste 120 #155
Durham, NC 27713
(984) 244-0250
benumedia.com

To receive special offers, release updates, and bonus content, sign up for our newsletter: go.benumedia.com/newsletter

ISBN (ebook): 978-1-7376311-1-8
ISBN (pbook): 978-1-7376311-2-5

Library of Congress Control Number: 2021918302

Cover Designer: Pintado (99Designs)
Editor: Jeni Chappelle (Jeni Chappelle Editorial)

Content Warnings

This book contains consensual on-page sex, physical violence, blood-drinking, on-page death, swearing, slurs (not toward any real racial or ethnic group/identity), alcohol use, threat of sexual violence, implied past sexual violence, and remembrance of a past abusive relationship.

It's also a steamy vampire romance with a happy ending, so make sure you have something to cool down with afterward!

For those who are trying their damnedest to find their place in the world when it feels like the rug has been pulled out from under them.

Chapter 1: Lya

Coming out of a vampire glamour was always one of the most disorienting experiences.

One minute, I was swimming in a reverie better than being drunk or high. The world was softened and muted. Nothing hurt. Euphoria smoothed all the rough edges in my brain. I could have quite literally died happy, which was entirely the idea.

The next minute, I was acutely aware of being watched by a predator, my body on high alert as I instinctively reacted to the threat. Adrenaline jarred through me, shooting tension through my muscles as the physical warred with the magical.

My eyes snapped open, and I found myself in a small bedroom decorated in bright fabrics that softened the walls of the underground space. The silk coverlet under me was soft, and the pillows were ridiculously fluffy. I tried to sit up, which resulted in more of a spasm.

I groaned as I realized the paralytic effect of the heavy glamour was still wearing off.

"There she is." My host sounded pleased with herself, as always.

I liked Maria though and didn't begrudge her the satisfaction. After all, our business arrangement—my blood in exchange for her protection—was what made it possible for a magic-wielding half-elf in exile like me to move freely in Raleigh.

As a bounty hunter, I needed to be able to pursue marks across the entire region without worrying about hungry vamps from Torsten's coterie making potentially deadly plays for me.

My full-blooded cousins were more or less required to stay in their territory in Chapel Hill unless they wanted to be someone's meal and strengthen one of their major competitors for power in the area. I had no power to lose, so for me, it was all upside. That the third most powerful vampire in town had a taste for elf blood was my lucky break, even if mine was thinner than my aforementioned cousins'.

"Morning," I mumbled when I was able, trying a smile.

"Not even." Maria's long, cobalt-colored tresses teased over the bare skin of my neck as she leaned over to inspect me. Her dark eyes searched mine as she inhaled, checking with all her senses that I was as well as could be expected, given that she'd taken at least a pint of blood. That blood gave her pale skin a rosy flush now. "Well. Technically, I suppose it is morning, but it's barely three. I told you you'd adjust, doll."

If I'd been together enough, my eyebrows would have shot up. The first time I'd let Maria glamour and bite me a few months ago, I'd been out from midnight to just past sunrise. We'd both gotten enough out of it to make it a regular thing. Coming back every six weeks through the winter and spring had kept up my access to Raleigh. It'd also kept my bank account full, as I was able to tag bounties the high-blood assholes in the Darkwatch didn't dare trespass for. Torsten, the vampire Master of Raleigh, had a short temper and a long memory when it came to uninvited trespassers. Especially elves or weres.

Mixed-bloods like me though, he didn't consider a threat. His mistake, Maria's benefit.

Maria was a rare forward-thinker among the vampires. Torsten was lucky to have her, even if I suspected he tended to overlook her. I also suspected that was her intention, given how harried Aron, the number two vamp in Raleigh, generally looked on the few occasions I'd glimpsed him.

I wrestled with the glamour. High-blood elves could use Aether to dispel a vampire's glamour from others but would fall into an alarmingly deep dissociative state without support. Low-bloods like me didn't fall quite so deep, and we healed a vampire bite faster than our high-blood cousins, given the human blend to our makeup. But it still hit us pretty hard. Some of us—*cough, cough*, yours truly—liked the occasional high of a glamour as an alternative to the chemical trips offered by drugs or alcohol. No hangover, even if it left you vulnerable to being drained. Slow-healing bites were a small price to pay, especially when I could mix business with pleasure.

I was an adrenaline junkie. So sue me.

It'd worked out in my favor so far. Since coming to North Carolina, at least.

Not so much back home.

Finally, I shook myself free of the last of the glamour. Maria had bandaged the wound she'd made in the bend of my elbow while I was out.

"Thanks," I said, flexing my left arm.

"Anytime. Especially if it means you come back for more. No pressure, of course." She smiled. "I should mention it's not just the glamour that's breaking faster. You're healing up better as well. Bite marks should be gone by tomorrow evening."

I grinned back at her and slid off the bed then caught myself as I swayed from sitting up too fast after the one-two punch of a glamour and a bite.

"Easy, doll."

"Yeah. No kidding. Same time in six weeks?"

"If you're offering, I won't say no." Maria tilted her chin down, peering up at me as she twirled a lock of hair around her finger.

I couldn't help but laugh. "Does anyone actually buy the innocent flirt routine?"

3

Her coffee-dark eyes flashed with amusement. "Most do. Unfortunately for them."

Shaking my head, I gave her a sloppy salute and made my way out. It wasn't the first time I'd left Maria's rooms in the basement of Claret, the wine bar she'd cultivated in a previously empty shop above the main entrance to the coterie's nest. We'd met when I'd wandered in looking for info on a tag, not realizing it was a vamp-owned bar until she'd sidled up to me and asked for a word in private. I'd thought the metaphysical power signature hanging over the place just meant there was a vampire city master nearby, not actually in residence, so it was good luck Maria had spotted me before someone more powerful.

Noah eyed me as I slipped out the door to her chambers but didn't hassle me. I couldn't figure out the relationship between him and Maria, but he was awfully protective of her. He also seemed to take orders from her. A fledgling, maybe, and a reasonably old one; his deep golden skin suggested he'd been born much darker than he was now and had spent a long time avoiding the sun.

Regardless, it wasn't really my business. I nodded to him and took the spiral stairs back up to the main floor more slowly than usual, mindful of my current state. The bar was busy when I pushed through the curtain hiding the narrow hallway ending in the door that led downstairs. *Indy Week* had done a feature on the place a few days ago, and the slow but consistent trickle of business had sped up considerably.

The vampires had a steady flow of potential donors now, and none of the mundanes even knew it.

Humans spoke too loudly over a nice jazz mix, and the scent of expensive wine filled the space. A few men I took to be single eyed me. One tried to catch my attention. I winked and kept walking, not interested in fucking a mundane tonight. I had nothing against them. My father was one, after all. But I'd

4

inherited more than the usual of my mother's Aetheric magic, and that meant I had to be more careful than I cared to be, given I'd been glamoured myself this evening. One slip and I could find myself breaking the Détente.

I shuddered at the idea of being hauled up in front of Callista. Nobody knew what flavor of Othersider the local boss was, but she was nasty as fuck and quick to deal out harsh punishments in the basement of her weird little bar up in Durham. I steered clear and minded my business like a good little low-blood, even if I resented the second-class status my human half gave me in Otherside—especially with my cousins.

Warm night air with just a hint of humidity greeted me as I slipped out of Claret. Early June was a good time to be in North Carolina, with reasonably comfortable nighttime temps and humidity on the lower end. This was the early side of hurricane season, although not many big storms made it this far inland at any strength to do more than flood the area. I was still settling into my exile after just under a year, but as exile went, this wasn't bad.

For the most part.

I was still able to do the work I enjoyed. I missed the cosmopolitan vibe of Europe, but the Triangle—as the locals called the trio of cities—was nowhere near as bad as my mother's House thought it'd be when they'd sent me to live with my distant cousins.

Or hell, maybe I should give myself some credit. Maybe I was just that good at adapting to shitty circumstances that weren't my fault.

I shook off the familiar rage before it could build into a fury that would send me looking for more of the trouble that'd gotten me exiled to begin with and booked an Uber back to Southpoint, ignoring the men giving me long glances and some not-quite-muttered compliments from where they waited in the queue outside Claret.

Finally, my Uber pulled up. The driver was a chatterbox all the damn way home. I let him talk, giving enough of a noncommittal sound to indicate agreement or outrage as seemed appropriate while I thought about what I was doing here in North Carolina. Something about tonight had me realizing I'd fallen into a pattern.

Patterns were dangerous. Doubly so for exiles like me, living at the very margins of my patrons' protection.

After I'd fucked up back home, House Monteague had authorized my transfer to the Triangle in exchange for the use of my skills as a bounty hunter—not that we called it that here, at least not where mundanes could hear.

Some state law that said you could *be* a bounty hunter but not call yourself one. Ridiculous.

Anything the local elven Houses couldn't or didn't want to use the Darkwatch for, they kicked to me. Sometimes I actually did play bond bail runner or process server for both Otherside and the mundanes, just to stay busy and keep money coming in.

Sometimes my work got quite a bit more exciting.

So far, it'd worked out.

So far. I wasn't naive enough to think that'd last forever, especially given the growing animosity between me and my boss, Farand.

When I say animosity, I mean the bigoted dick hated me for being good at my job despite being a low-blood. Which meant I needed a backup plan. I'd thought Maria was it, but the more I thought, the more I realized it was just another distraction from the loneliness that kept me up at night sometimes. Another routine.

I hated routine.

The driver slowed as we hit the off-ramp at Southpoint.

Shaking free of my thoughts, I sat up and leaned forward. "Right off the exit and then through the light. Then left into the shopping center at the next light. You can drop me in the Tobacco Trail parking. Thanks."

Chatterbox frowned at me in the rearview mirror. "It's not safe on the trail this time of night, ma'am. Last week there was a—"

"I know, but I'll be fine. Thanks for your concern." I'd rather take my chances with the occasional asshole on the trail after dark than with someone definitely knowing where I lived. At five-eight, lean, and pretty, I knew I looked like bait. The knife sheathed on my forearm under my light jacket, the Walther PPK in my purse, and the frequent experience of using them said otherwise, even if I hadn't had just enough control of Aether to sting a would-be attacker and magically suggest they fuck right off.

With a shrug, the driver did as I'd asked.

I slid out of the car then waited for him to pull away before heading west along the trail. Technically it was "south," but this part curved around the upscale strip mall on the northern side of NC-54, giving people a quieter path to follow than the busy road. The gates at the entry of the community stopped cars, but walking a little took me to the end of the fencing and the fountain that indicated where my unit was—a serious security failure in my estimation, but I hadn't chosen the place.

With a quick look around, I cut across the lawn and around to the front of the building, avoiding the geese giving me the evil eye as they shuffled to get between me and their young. The only noise came from an idling semi parked up at the Harris Teeter, dropping off a restock. I hated the constant noise from traffic coming down Fayetteville and 54, but it was another layer of security. If my family got sick of the disgrace of my exile and a triad of Darkwatch elves came for me and tried using a soundproofing spell to kill me quietly in my sleep, the absence of sound would tip me off.

For now though, the stillness of my one-bed apartment was kind of depressing.

The bells swinging from the inside doorknob clattered as I shut the door and locked it, another insurance policy. A bounty hunter could never be too careful. If a tag got wind of me before I could strike or if a high-blood took exception to my presence or any of the dozens of things that could go wrong in Otherside went wrong, I wanted a warning.

You're too fucking paranoid.

I shoved the mental voice aside and scrubbed my hands over my face. Paranoid kept me alive. It also kept me lonely.

Idle flirtation aside, my deal with Maria was strictly business. I'd been in town long enough now to learn who held territory where, who not to fuck with, and who could be bought, and I was starting to feel the itch.

Fortunately, I was closing in on a bounty. If I could bring her in tomorrow, I could afford to take a night off and celebrate. Maybe find a little company for the evening.

A night off in someone's arms couldn't hurt, right? Especially since I'd been such a good—and lonely—girl since arriving in town. Keeping my head down, doing my job, not ruffling any feathers.

Yeah. It was my turn to have a little fun. All I had to do was get this one job done.

Bringing in a werewolf who was in the territory without permission was one of those jobs that was too small for the Darkwatch to dirty their hands with and too politically sensitive for the local wereleopard leap to handle themselves.

Still, I thanked the Goddess when we—my bounty and I— got to the storefront Callista had set up as a bond agency in Durham without incident the next morning.

My boss looked up, his dark brows lifting in surprise and his mouth twisting into a condescending smile as he saw me marching the were, Viktoria Volkov, in ahead of me. "Another tag. Somehow you continue to impress, Desmarais. Keep this up, and you might actually come off probation one day."

I gritted my teeth. Farand was a Monteague, and while he might be from the lesser branch of the House, it was still the most powerful one in the Triangle. Its queen had a particular dislike of anyone not pure-blood elf, so while I was *useful*, that didn't mean I was *valued*.

Viktoria watched the exchange with too-clever blue eyes but said nothing. We'd had a solid talk in the car on the way over.

I flushed with embarrassment before I could remind myself that Farand's bullshit was nothing to do with anything that was my fault. Forcing a tight smile of my own, I said, "Where do you want her?"

He tilted her head to the chair next to his desk, and Viktoria went and sat without being told, pulling her brown ponytail over her shoulder.

"Good dog," Farand murmured, a nasty twist to his lips and tone. He was always doing this kind of shit to me and anyone else he thought was beneath him.

Viktoria stiffened, glancing at me for some reason.

I shook my head. *Not worth it, girl. Let this one go.*

Blessedly, the small but fiery werewolf listened. It made Farand's attitude even more unbearable.

This time I had to remind myself it wouldn't be worth it to slap the smug bastard. *A big drink*, I promised myself. *Better yet, a whole bottle of prosecco just for me and whoever tickles my fancy tonight in my bed. I can always encourage them to forget if I slip up with the magic.*

Just to piss Farand off, I nodded to Viktoria. "Thank you for your cooperation, miss. I'll be sure Terrence hears of it for consideration in your sentencing."

The werewolf's eyes widened slightly, then she gathered herself and nodded. "I'd appreciate that."

With a last tight smile, I spun on my heel and left before Farand could instigate something that'd get me exiled for a second time.

I fumed as I headed back home after getting Volkov's car sorted for her return to Asheville. I was worth more than this. I was better than this. But all these high-blood assholes saw was my mixed heritage and my heavy past. All I did was continually prove myself and my skills. If I didn't know any better, I'd been given the werewolf job with the expectation that I'd fuck it up. Everyone knew weres could be volatile, especially young ones this close to a full moon.

That idea froze the blood in my veins as I walked down the Tobacco Trail, not willing to go home just yet. Were they trying to get rid of me? For what? Being good enough—or better—despite my half-human heritage?

Anger drained from me as the old struggle reared its head. That shit. Again.

I just wanted someone to see me for me. Just one person. Someone who would appreciate my strengths without thinking my weaknesses or differences made me less-than. Someone had once, but he'd been too weak to stand up for the love he'd claimed when the shit hit the fan.

I was tired of it. Tired of living with the blame for things that weren't my fault. Tired of being either a tool or ignored. Tired of working my ass off to get crumbs. I loved the bounty hunting part of my job and my life but...not much else. I didn't have much of anything else.

It was time to change that.

I needed something for me. And yeah, the state's licensing requirements for bounty hunters might mean I had to stay with Farand's bond agency for another three months to maintain my mundane cover but after that? After that, I was a free agent. By mundane law, anyway. Farand hated me, so I couldn't imagine that he'd fight too hard to keep me if I decided to go freelance.

With a sudden burst of defiance, I knew where I'd go to celebrate tonight: back to Raleigh. Not to Claret but to a new club I'd read about a couple weeks ago. It looked classy, like the kind of scene I used to enjoy back in Lyon and London. Bonus: other elves wouldn't dare trespass there. I could use the protection my blood had bought from Maria and have a whole night free of the risk of running into my asshole cousins.

I needed to start thinking of my future, not my past. I couldn't go back home for a while, even if I was ready to forgive my family, so what was I going to do now that I was here? If I could make connections in the Triangle that few others could and move beyond the limitations set on full-blooded Othersiders, why not use that?

The more I thought about it, the more excited I got. I already had a vampire connection in Maria. She seemed the resourceful type. But I couldn't just let myself be tied to her, or I'd be in the same situation all over again.

Tonight had to be a hunt but a different sort than usual. I needed to network—and for the love of the Goddess, I needed to get laid. Make some kind of connection, however shallow, before loneliness had my social hormones in a full-on crash and I sank into the sort of depression the elf-blooded struggled to come out of.

Odds were that I'd end up with a human, but what if I bumped into a vampire willing to take a risk on a half-elf? I wouldn't let one glamour me for a one-night stand, but I'd been wondering for ages whether all those years of life had translated into skill in the bedroom.

It was past time to find out.

Chapter 2: Cade

Cade sprawled in the dark corner booth of the latest of Raleigh's watering holes to be bought out by Torsten's coterie. This one was a little more upscale, more to his tastes for hunting than the wine bar that'd started Maria's experimental foray into entertainment venues as a source of blood.

Popular music played a little too loudly for his vampiric senses, but the humans seemed to enjoy it. He surveyed them like a shark watching a school of fish as they swayed and flowed, shifting and navigating around each other. A minor glamour effect kept them from being unsettled by his presence and would make them overlook his fangs if he slipped up, not that he had in a long, long time.

He was old enough now to do better. Still, one couldn't be too careful.

He'd had high hopes for this club. Dressed his best, in a tailored, three-piece suit. Wore his best watch. A little overdone, but he always preferred to go over than under.

All the same, he'd been sat here since sundown, an untouched whiskey neat in front of him, waiting for something interesting. Some*one* interesting. A gaggle of women had approached him, and he'd taken a few sips of blood from each of them under the guise of a dance before healing the bite, glamouring them into forgetfulness, and sending them on their merry way.

Cade huffed a sigh. This was *surviving*. He had what he needed, but he wanted more. Something that felt like living. Like *thriving*.

No. More like power.

He'd been in hiding for years, not using any of the advantages his age offered, shifting from city to city rather than tying himself to a coterie. After the horrors of his first two and a half centuries, freedom and movement had felt like safety.

Cade still wanted safety, but he was starting to feel like it was time for a change in how he achieved it—which was why he was still in Raleigh after eighteen months. The unusual power structure here, with the local coterie balanced by an elven conclave and a joined werecat pride under an Arbiter who ruled rather than simply advising, afforded unusual opportunity to source powerful blood with less risk.

He schooled himself to patience as he reminded himself that the night was barely half over. Time yet for his luck to change.

Movement caught his eye. Not just movement. Presence.

Cade tracked the newcomer as she moved through the room. Slightly above average height for a woman. Built like she practiced martial arts as her workout plan, with cleanly defined muscles and easy movement that said she knew her body. Loose curls were cut short on the back and sides but left to their wild abundance on top, falling to her jaw on one side. A roving spotlight passed over her, illuminating the shimmery gold halter top that complimented her terra-cotta brown skin and the snake tattoo twining around her left arm. Sharp brown eyes scanned the room, lighting up when she spotted the bar.

Humans moved out of her way without seeming to notice they'd done so, seamlessly closing the gap when she passed.

She was an Othersider. Had to be. Not a vampire—he'd met all the locals by now and hadn't heard of any recent arrivals.

Which meant someone might be trespassing on vampire territory.

A smile curled Cade's lips. This was worth investigating. He had protections as a vagabond. But non-vampires in Torsten's territory? Fair game for the taking. What luck, with Cade in the market for more powerful blood than what these humans had to offer.

If it came in a package that looked like it could beat his ass, so much the better. He loved a challenge.

The blood he'd already taken earlier rushed through his veins as his heart beat faster at the prospect of a hunt worth undertaking. He didn't need more tonight, but a connection made now could be sipped from later.

He slipped through the crowd, the mundanes parting for him much as they had for his target but paying him more notice. A few people offered him admiring smiles. One woman went so far as to trail a hand over his chest.

"Another time, beautiful." Cade put a light push of glamour behind the words as he caught her eyes, and she pouted but went back to dancing.

His target eyed him as he approached and leaned on the bar beside her. The bartender was popping a fresh bottle of prosecco, and a flute was in front of the Othersider.

"Yours?" Cade asked, nodding to the drink. She just flashed her brows, so he took that as a yes. The slight parting of her lips as she took his measure encouraged him. "Put anything this lady wants on my tab, Philip. Leave the bottle."

The vampire bartender glanced at the woman, waiting for her nod to say, "Certainly, sir."

"Exploring the other side tonight?" Cade asked.

Her eyebrows lifted. "I had you pegged from the second I hit the floor, but most of you don't notice little old me. What gave it away?"

14

Cade offered a small, secretive smile. "Live long enough and you learn a few tricks. I'm Cade."

"Lya."

He brought the hand she boldly extended to his lips, not quite kissing it, and enjoyed the quick tightening and relaxing of her features as she evaluated whether he was greeting her or attacking her. More, he enjoyed the faint whiff of rosemary, sage, and meringue he caught from her hand. Elf. Low-blood but close enough to Otherside to work Aether. With that accent, a traveler without House connections to tell her where not to go or an exile nobody would miss. Perfect.

Hunting high-blood elves was a quick way to start an inter-factional incident that would get that bitch Callista involved, but low-bloods who strayed from the safety of their territory were fair game by virtue of being human-blooded.

With one of his more disarming smiles, Cade said, "Join me?"

"Seeing as you're buying, why the hell not."

Confident. He liked that. A lot. She had to know what he was, being in this part of the Triangle—and it wasn't like he was going easy on the glamour either. Cade's new question was whether it was because she had a more powerful backer or because she was confident she could handle a vampire. Or both.

A worthwhile challenge.

He snagged the ice-filled bucket and the second glass Philip had left, leading this mystery woman back to his table. They settled into the booth, knees bumping in a way Cade suspected was purposeful on Lya's part from the flirty look she gave him.

"Before we get this party started, I have one ground rule," she said after she toasted him and sipped her drink.

"And that is?"

Her smile stopped his heart and froze the stolen blood in his veins, equal parts mischief and violence as she touched her purse in a meaningful way. "If you try to glamour or drink from me,

I'll cut your balls off and force feed them to you. I can be very convincing when it comes to bouncers, and I don't come to Raleigh without silver."

Cade mentally thanked Hekate for sending this delightful hellion his way. With a smile that matched hers, he slowly reached out to cup her jaw. Her expression hardened even as she carefully avoided his eyes, and he lightly ran a thumb over her lower lip. "I don't take Othersiders without their consent and humans only as necessary to hunt, feed, or maintain the Détente." He let that sink in then leaned closer to whisper in her ear as he let his hand slip to her neck. "Besides, why would I force a glamour on you when it'd be so much more fun to make you beg for it?"

The pulse under his fingers sped up. "It takes a lot to make me beg."

"Is that a challenge?"

Finally, she met his gaze. Lya's pupils had dilated, and Cade suppressed the urge to pull her under, determined to win by the rules he'd just set. Something hungry swam up behind her eyes.

"Give it your best shot," she said.

"As my lady commands. Shall we dance?" Cade rose, extending a hand.

His pulse restarted at the quick flash of delight in her expression before she downed the rest of her prosecco, shaking her head at the bubbles, then took it. He pulled her out to the dance floor, pleased when she spun to press her back to his front and began moving to the music in a way that made his cock stir.

His earlier consideration to let her slip away unfucked and untasted shattered as she moved against him. Lya made the blood throb through him like the music did, even before she bent forward and ground that sweet, tight ass against his crotch. When he ran a finger down her spine, she snapped upright and slithered down his front, brushing his cock on her way down and back up in a way that was maddeningly direct.

"You're going to kill me a second time." Cade gripped her hips to keep her in place and give him a break for one Goddess-damned minute. Humans were never this sure of their bodies, this joyful in their movements, and he hadn't been with an Othersider in at least half a century.

Lya just swiveled her hips, arching back to kiss the corner of his jaw. Her breath sent tingles over his skin as she replied, "Keep up, old man."

"You saucy little minx." He spun her, pressing her body into his with a hand splayed at the small of her back before lowering his lips to her neck and teasing himself by gently nibbling with his incisors.

Rather than being scared by the possible threat of his sharp canines, the woman laughed.

Laughed, a bubbling of sound that turned heads.

The scent of lust spiked in the immediate area.

Cade pulled away and gave her a spin before pulling her back to him. "Let's sit down before you cause a riot."

Before I break my word and bite you here and now.

Amusement sparkled in her gaze as though she could hear his unspoken thought, but she allowed him to lead her back to their table. She poured herself another glass of prosecco, nodding at his empty one. "You're not having any?"

"I could. But no."

"That old, huh?"

Cade just smiled at the hint of wariness that realization sparked, glad that she wasn't a complete fool. Fools were boring, too easy to use and discard. Otherside blood offered power, but so did intelligence.

All vampires could hypothetically eat or drink anything they wanted. They still had human physiology, after all. But the virus that gave them long life, accelerated healing, and supernatural senses and reflexes was best sustained by avoiding anything that accelerated cellular degeneration or destruction: sunlight, fire, refined carbs, alcohol, and so on. Blood had the optimal proteins and nutrients to sustain the virus, so blood was what they subsisted on to keep their undead systems running as long as possible.

Not that they told the rest of Otherside that, allowing them all to believe that only the oldest vampires, those who'd reached a level high enough to be sent to negotiations with other factions, could eat or drink anything other than blood.

Lya studied him as she sipped her bubbly. "Your self-control is encouraging."

"You were testing me?"

Again, the flash of eyebrows signaling a yes as she took another sip.

"What would you have done if I'd slipped?"

"Made you regret it." She smiled again, that blend of deviltry and seduction that made him want to pin her to the padded bench they were sitting on and have her in front of everyone.

That piqued his interest further. "Your cousins are arrogant fucks, but they have the sense not to tease one of us."

"My cousins are boring. Me, I like a little excitement in my life." Another up-and-down look. She finished her prosecco and set it aside before sliding closer to him, running a hand under his suit jacket as she leaned closer to whisper. "If it's too much for you, I can always go find someone else to play with."

"No." Something almost like desperation ripped through him. Cade wanted this woman all to himself. Tonight, preferably. Soon, if she slipped him.

Boldly, she met his eyes again. "You sure?"

"Yes." He swallowed, trying to get his raging lust under control before he made an ass of himself. *Fuck it.* "I want to kiss you."

"Then do it."

Forcing himself not to use his full strength to cup her jaw and press his lips to hers was the hardest thing he'd done all night, especially when she skimmed her hand up his body again and dragged her nails down his neck.

When he growled a warning, she groaned. Her tongue darted over his lips, brushing tantalizingly past his canines. It didn't count as biting her if she cut herself, did it? But she didn't, somehow taking control of the kiss he'd initiated with a skill that made his already hard cock ache even more.

When they broke for air, Cade was flustered enough to actually need to breathe.

"You're a damn tease," he said hoarsely.

"You have potential," she shot back.

"Just potential?"

"Mmm…maybe a little more than that." Her gaze darted down to the evidence of his interest, making a bulge in his expensive trousers. With a smirk, she said, "I'll be right back."

Lya threaded through the crowd toward the ladies' restroom. He didn't miss the way she shook herself, as though coming down from a high. All he could hope was that the feeling she kindled in him was mutual.

Leaning back in the corner of the booth, he tilted his head back and tried to find calm again. Cade prided himself on slow, controlled hunts where he drove his prey to desperation. A little sadistic, maybe, but he never pushed beyond what was explicitly asked for.

This time, he feared he might be the one begging.

Chapter 3: Lya

I took a deep breath as I looked at myself in the mirror then another one when I still felt shaky. It wasn't drunkenness—I could handle a lot more booze than I'd had.

It was Cade.

Even without glamour, he did something to me. It wasn't the British accent reminding me of my second home in London or the impeccable sweep of his dark hair or the way his eyes, startlingly dark alongside his pale skin, seemed to see straight into my core. The frisson of excitement that ran over me at the sense of contained danger I got from him was part but not all of it.

Shaking my head, I dug around in my purse. Checked that I still had my knives. Those had needed a little push of Aether to get past the human bouncer, but I wasn't going to risk being unarmed in Raleigh. I fished out the eyeliner nestled next to them and touched up the smudge at the corner of one eye then swiped a tinted balm over my lips.

I'd come down to Raleigh hoping to find a vampire and might have gotten more than I'd wished for.

Of course, there was only one way to find out.

The smart choice would be to call it a night. But I didn't want to. I was enjoying myself for once, and it was thawing the icy loneliness at my core. I still had to pay attention, and it wasn't exactly clever to bait a vampire the way I had been. But he'd been a gentleman so far.

Did I trust him to have me alone somewhere?

I shivered at the idea, thinking back to the impressive hint of what was in his trousers. The strength of his hands as they gripped my hips, the nibble along my neck. The way my core had clenched at the thought of how he might get me to beg to be glamoured.

Damn it.

"Be smart, Lya," I muttered to myself as I packed everything up. But what was I trading blood to Maria for if not for leverage in situations like this? I could do this—do him—but I needed another test.

Then it hit me. Grinning, I used the facilities and then headed back to his table.

Cade watched me approach with the laser focus of the predator he was then wrapped an arm over my shoulder as I slid close to him. "Everything okay?"

"Everything's fab."

"Still enjoying your night out?"

I skimmed a hand over his thigh, enjoying the way he shifted up into my touch with the smallest movement of his hips. "Definitely. In fact, I was wondering if you wanted to get out of here and go somewhere quieter."

A rich chuckle gave me chills. "Looking to have a more private party?"

"With the right company."

"You're not worried I'll take advantage of you?"

"I think you'll do whatever I want you to do." At his sharp intake of breath, I tilted to nibble his neck as he had mine on the dance floor. "And absolutely nothing more. At least, that's how it'd better be."

His hands fisted as he tilted his head back. "Lya, I don't know if you're brazen or foolish to play this hard with me. Maybe both."

I agreed, but it wasn't like I was going to say so, not when I was so close to finally getting the night I'd come here looking for. "Is that a no to moving this party then?"

Tilting his head, he kissed me again, deeper than before.

This time, his tongue explored my mouth as his hand toyed with the edge of my skirt.

When I shifted to let his fingers dip underneath, he squeezed my thigh and pulled away.

"There are VIP rooms here," he said. "If you like."

"I do like." Even easier than a hotel. "As long as you stay the gentleman and I don't have to call on my local friend."

"I'll go have a word with Philip." He rose a little too quickly for human, shaking his head as he checked himself and walked to the bar at a more measured pace. After a word with the bartender I'd noted was a vampire, he clapped the man's shoulder and pocketed something.

I poured myself more prosecco and sipped it, watching him return as he'd watched me.

"Shall we?" He extended a hand.

I took it and rose. "Before we do, I meant what I said about having friends in town, got it?"

"Understood. But you have nothing to fear from me." Cade grabbed the bucket and led me to a staircase I'd noted coming in. He nodded at the bouncer leaning on the wall alongside it, and the man nodded back.

That's when I clocked it: the venue was owned by vampires, not just staffed by them. Clever move on someone's part. Probably Maria's, given that Claret was hers.

At the top of the stairs was a short, dark hallway with a few numbered doors. My heart pounded as Cade unlocked one then led me in and set the prosecco bucket on the table next to an unobtrusive box. After a quick glance around to make sure the room was empty aside from us, I gasped at the view that greeted me out the floor-to-ceiling windows.

Raleigh glittered below. A small balcony outside a sliding glass door said we could take this outside if we wanted, and heavy blackout curtains at either end said we could go past dawn.

I turned to inspect the rest of the room. Low, comfortable-looking couches made right angles to bracket the similarly low table now holding the ice bucket. Oversized cushions offered seating on the other two edges. In another corner, a loveseat sat in an arrangement with two armchairs and a small table. Music from the club played at a quieter level through hidden speakers.

Two doors were in the far wall. I checked them, finding a bathroom with an exquisite mosaic tiling the floor and a claw-foot bathtub, then a windowless bedroom with one of the biggest beds I'd ever seen. On one wall were some intriguing implements that we wouldn't be trying out tonight but had possibility if he behaved and I was daring enough to do this again.

Cade waited for me to inspect everything, his gaze on me as he leaned against the thick windows.

"This is nice." I finished my bubbly and set the glass next to the bucket on the table. "Everything's lightproof? Soundproof?"

"Yes to both, in case one of us loses track of time or our guests get enthusiastic."

"Or someone wants to have a private orgy? That bed is massive."

With a grin, Cade shrugged. "We're practical like that."

"Do something practical with your mouth then." The words tumbled out before I could think about them, but I tilted my chin up as though I'd planned to make demands.

His smile turned wicked. "As my lady commands."

I couldn't take my eyes off him as he approached slowly, almost like a lion stalking prey in high grass. "Afraid I'm going to run?"

"A little."

"You planning to hurt me?"

"Only if you ask for it and only what you ask for, until you tell me to stop. You're in charge, Lya. I'm your humble servant. For now. But if you want to play, we play with all of us. As Othersiders."

My heart skipped a beat then raced at what that meant.

No hiding. No holding back, except for the boundaries we agreed to.

Whatever that did to my scent, it hit him like a slap from the way he paused, eyelashes fluttering, and rolled his head to make a vertebra pop. Again his control reassured me—and sent the heat in me spiking higher.

"Agreed," I said breathily. "No glamour. No bloodletting. Nothing that leaves a mark."

When he spoke next, his voice was rough as smoke and heavy as fog. "Agreed. Ready or not, here I come."

Before I could react, Cade moved. I barely saw him before he'd closed the distance between us, grabbed me, and spun me to put my back to the window, my wrists pinned over my head. He kicked my feet wide and pressed his body full-length against mine.

I gasped, instinctively twisting in a move that should have broken his grip. He didn't budge, and the way I was trapped meant I couldn't kick him.

I still tried my damnedest.

"I thought you must be a martial artist." He sounded pleased he'd been right, not mocking. Still, he just stood there, waiting for me to decide whether I found this frightening or hot.

My brain whirled. What the fuck was I doing playing games like this with a vampire old enough that he could drink booze?

If he wanted me dead, I'd be dead. Right now.

His teeth would be in my throat before I could scream and the room's soundproofing meant nobody would hear. Maria's protection might as well be on the moon.

"Lya?"

"What?" I said in a shuddering voice.

"Are we stopping or going?"

I held my breath to get it under control. He wasn't attacking me, either to bite or to force something sexually, never mind that he was still hard as a damn iron rod.

He was waiting for me to be okay. To direct him.

Cade was still in control, which meant I was in control.

If I wasn't going to die, I liked it. "Go."

"You're sure?"

I tilted my head up and brushed my lips along his jaw. "Yes."

"Good."

His lips fell on mine, claiming me all over again. He changed his grip on my wrists to be one handed, teasing the other down my flank. Questing fingers teased along the hem of my shirt.

"May I?" he whispered against my lips.

"You can take it off, if you lose the jacket and shirt."

"Don't go anywhere," he said sternly, letting go of my wrists.

I leaned against the window, enjoying the sight of him stripping. And it was a strip: a slow, languorous shedding of clothing. The jacket and waistcoat, he tossed on one of the couches. The shirt followed after he'd opened it button by button, never taking his eyes off me. I drank in the sight of smooth planes of muscle, recognizing a form that'd been gained through labor, not gym time. It was hard to tell in the dark, but it looked like a few scars dotted him.

"Satisfied?" he asked.

"You're going to have to work a lot harder than that."

"I plan to."

With the same slow movements he'd used to undress himself, he shimmied my close-fitting top over my head. I lifted my arms to oblige him and was rewarded with his mouth, hot and damp, as he first kissed then sucked on my nipple through the thin lace of my bra. He teased the other nipple with one hand and kept me pressed against the window with a light grip around my throat after he dropped the shirt.

As long as I didn't move, there was no pressure. But the pull of his mouth and fingers made me press into his hand. Then his grip forced me to be still, only for me to arch back up again as he pulled harder. I couldn't help the whimper that escaped me as I gripped his waist.

"That's what I like to hear."

My "shut up" was more strangled by pleasure than his hand, but he eased up anyway.

"Don't stop," I breathed, flushing at how much I really, really didn't want him to. All thoughts of danger were gone. I'd gone untouched, unwanted, for so fucking long.

"Not planning on it." Keeping me pinned to the window, he reached for the hem of my skirt next.

"Yes," I panted before he could ask. "Something. Give me something, you—"

Cade kissed me again as he ran a hand between my thighs with a caress that seemed to explode in my brain. I groaned into his mouth, the sound becoming guttural as he slid my panties to the side and slipped his fingers along my well-moistened folds. My knees almost gave out as he found my pearl and rubbed it.

"You smell so damn good," he whispered against my neck. "Can I give you a little more?"

I almost stammered out a "please" then bit it back as I remembered what he'd said about begging. "Yes."

26

The word had barely left my mouth before he sank a finger between my lower lips. A second joined it, and they both curled to move back and forth over that spot.

My hands strayed to the bulge in the front of his trousers, imagining him inside me. "Fuck, Cade. Fuck."

"Soon. If you're good and come for me now."

If I hadn't been on the edge of an orgasm, I'd have had something to say about that, but all that came out of my mouth was a groan as I went over the edge.

His hands shifted, and then he carried me to one of the couches. Cool air made my nipples stand up as he took off my bra. I fumbled for his belt, desperate for more of him. He let me do it, focusing on kissing my neck and breasts again. The barest prick of sharp teeth drew a gasp from me, and he paused but kept going when I yanked his belt loose and went for the button and fly.

No blood, no foul.

"How far do you want this to go?" Cade's voice sounded as ragged as I felt.

"How long do we have the room?"

"All night. There are condoms in the box on the table, if you want them."

Vampires couldn't get anyone pregnant, and the vamp virus aggressively killed off any other microbes that might try to colonize their bodies. But a condom made cleanup so much easier. "I do."

Normally I would've been annoyed at the presumption— renting a VIP room for the whole night? Just for us? But tonight I was glad. I was getting everything I'd hoped for and then some, without having to risk going to a hotel or wherever he nested. I'd worry about the possible business angle in the morning.

Right now, an incredibly sexy vampire was standing up to tug his pants off and then his briefs, freeing a cock that was exactly what I'd imagined from feeling him up.

Cade rolled a condom over himself with vampiric speed and then was back on top of me, somehow even more passionate than before—his touch rougher, his kisses with more of a nip to them, his nails digging in a little more as he dragged my skirt and panties down. "Sure you don't want to call it a night?"

I found him and guided him into me. "Certain."

He buried his face in my neck as he pushed deeper, taking it slow to let me get used to the feel of him. There was a lot to take, and I was glad of the warm-up.

When I was ready, I pushed my hips up into his and squeezed his ass. "Fuck me."

Cade didn't bother with a smart quip this time. He just caught my wrists and pinned them over my head again then moved with easy power, smooth and unhurried, shifting until I cried out in pleasure and bucked against him, needing more. Then he sped up, staying where he was to hit the same spot every time, over and over, until I was practically sobbing his name, lost in ecstasy.

"Come for me." The growl of his voice in my ear was accompanied by a shift in his grip from my wrists to my neck, the same light pressure to either side of my throat as before.

It sent me over the edge. I dragged my nails down his back as I obeyed, my body fighting to arch up and being held in place by his.

Cade's grip tightened as he followed me with animalistic grunts.

When we'd both finished, he shifted just enough to take his weight off me and pull off the condom before rolling back to spoon me. The couch was just wide enough for it.

"The bed would be more comfortable," I said. Having had that taste of him, I wanted more. If we had the whole night, that was what I wanted. I had a chance to get everything I needed and then some, and I was damn well going to take it.

"You know what? I think you're right."

I shrieked as he was upright and had me over his shoulder fast as a thought then laughed as he dumped me on the bed and resumed our previous position.

For a while, I luxuriated in high thread-count sheets and the feeling of being held. As my heart rate slowed back to normal though, my body craved more. "Will you be up for another round tonight?"

Kisses danced from the nape of my neck to the curve of my shoulder. "Absolutely."

"Then it's my turn to return the favor."

Cade's grip tightened on me, and I grinned at my ideas for the night ahead.

Chapter 4: Lya

I woke the next morning sprawled in a bed that smelled mostly of the ash and iron of vampire, with an undercurrent of granite, a hint of my own herby scent, and a lot of sex.

Shit.

Spending the night was not like me. Definitely not in the rented bed of a vampire I'd just met. I glanced over my shoulder, biting back a groan for the muscles that felt like I'd done a few rounds in the ring.

Cade was sprawled on his back next to me, not seeming to breathe. He would be, just at a rate that was so slow it'd be imperceptible. It was still unnerving.

I shifted and eased to the edge of the bed, halted by a gentle grip on my wrist.

He inhaled deeply. "Let me guess. You don't usually spend the night."

The sleep-heavy rumble of his voice sent a jolt through me, but I still shook my head. "Um. No. I don't."

I was a little embarrassed that I had, but…I'd needed this.

He tugged lightly on my wrist. I could have broken free, but memories of last night flashed through my mind. *Fuck it.* I let him draw me closer until I was straddling him. His skin was cool and dry as I indulged myself in running my hands over the sharp definition of his muscles and the ridges of scars. He'd been cut several times and shot at least once while he was alive, but that could mean anything.

Dark eyes opened just enough to regard me as he settled his hands on my hips. "Does that mean you're not coming back?"

I pursed my lips and pretended to think about it before leaning forward and nibbling at his throat. The surprised growl I pulled from him heated my blood enough to make me consider staying for some morning fun, but he'd probably have to bite me for that to happen. I didn't let one-night stands bite.

"I might," I whispered in his ear.

Cade squeezed my hips and shifted to grind against me slightly. "I'd like to see you again."

I snorted and pulled away. "I bet you would."

"Not just for the chance at a bite." He studied me, looking almost confused. "This was...unexpectedly fun."

I couldn't help laughing. "You know what? Likewise."

Before I could let myself be seduced into more, I slid off of him and hunted down my clothes. His gaze weighed on me as I dressed, but he didn't try to change my mind. Points to him.

"Can I get you a cab?" he asked.

I waved my phone. "I'll get an Uber."

With a stretch that had only a little of the clockwork jerkiness of an unfed vampire, he reached for the wallet on his nightstand and pulled out a bill. "Can't let it be said I didn't do what I could to get a date home."

I hesitated before stepping closer to accept it. A spark of laughter lit his dark gaze as he clearly read my readiness to jump away if he tried to grab me, and he settled back on the pillows when I had the bill.

"Thanks." I swallowed a wave of desire. He wasn't trying to glamour me. He was just that hot.

"Give me a minute to get dressed, and I'll wait with you."

"No need." I wanted to get the hell out and get some fresh air.

He'd been good last night, but he had to be hungry now. I told myself I needed to go because he was more dangerous now, but mostly I wanted distance from the man busy looking deliciously fuckable before I stripped and offered my throat for more of what we'd done last night. I think he could tell, from the knowing smile curing his lips.

"Right. Thanks for everything," I said.

I let myself out of the VIP room, surprised all over again that we were aboveground, although that was exactly what the heavy blackout curtains were for. Sunlight wouldn't kill a vampire outright, although it was terribly uncomfortable for them and would eventually do enough cellular damage that the virus they carried couldn't repair it. Most vamps preferred to take the precaution of living underground, but it seemed Cade was happy to live dangerously.

A man after my own heart.

Different staff than had been in last night glanced at me as I hurried down the stairs.

I nodded to them and said, "Thanks. Nice rooms."

The bartender just gave me a sleepy smirk. I rushed out of the club and to the lift, face hot, tapping my foot as I waited and beating myself up for being stupid. It was easier to see—easier to think—now that I was out of Cade's intoxicating presence.

It'd had nothing to do with the prosecco. I knew myself and how I behaved while drinking. It couldn't have been drugged either. My training back home had been very thorough, and I knew what that felt like. Being half-elven, I would have needed a much bigger dose than a human as well, one that would have knocked me down hard.

No, I was standing here looking for and discarding excuses because, for once, I'd gotten exactly what I'd come looking for.

Not only had it not bitten me in the ass or anywhere else, I'd also *liked* it. I'd *enjoyed* myself, in a way that felt forbidden and luscious and not meant for me, the half-blooded bastard child partway in the world of Otherside but partway in the world of the mundanes.

But why shouldn't I have enjoyed it?

The lift finally arrived, and the whole way down, I sorted through my feelings. I didn't feel guilty because I'd done something foolish and spent the night with a vampire in a club's VIP kink room. I'd spent my life doing wild shit my family nearly always frowned upon, like becoming a bounty hunter to begin with.

I felt guilty because I'd dared to claim something nice for myself.

And I could do it again. Cade had made that abundantly clear.

I couldn't shake the thrill that idea sent through me as the Uber whisked me back to Southpoint. The hundred-dollar bill I found in my hand when I unclenched it didn't hurt Cade's chances either. I wasn't above taking a man's cash if he wanted to hand it out. Farand paid me at a lower rate than his other bond runners, despite the fact that I could do jobs the rest of his runners couldn't do. He knew it, I knew it, they knew it, and because they were high-bloods, there wasn't shit I could do about it as long as I was required to abide by the terms of my exile here.

My plan from yesterday came back. I still had a few months left before I could go freelance as a bounty hunter and work for hire, rather than as an indenture. Would the vampires help me once I did? Did I dare ask? They seemed to want me around a hell of a lot more than the elves did.

Something to think about.

After I got home, I checked myself thoroughly when I stripped to shower, using a mirror to check anywhere I couldn't quite see.

As Cade had promised, he hadn't left a mark on me. Certainly not a bite but also not a hickey, nail scrape, or a bruise from fingers gripping tight in passion, despite the strength in his big hands. I flushed as I remembered biting him in pleasure and realized he wouldn't be able to say the same, but he hadn't set any boundaries and hadn't stopped me from doing anything. As enthusiastic as I'd gotten, he'd taken it all and dared me—commanded me, even—to give him more.

I shivered as more memories tripped through me. He'd stopped being careful to hide his fangs but still hadn't crossed the line I'd drawn, being himself without hurting me. I'd never been with anyone like that before. I couldn't be myself with humans, and I'd avoided most Othersiders because of the risk of harm. There'd been a few over the years but nothing like I'd experienced last night with Cade.

That's why he's dangerous.

The side of my brain that saw that fact and understood he might just be trying to lure me was warning me to stay away from the vampire.

The part of me that drank up being seen and desired and flat-out worshipped demanded more. It wasn't just my blood that was on fire at the memory of last night; it was my soul as well.

Then there was my arrangement with Maria. She hadn't made exclusivity or sex a part of the deal. We weren't dating, and I didn't belong to her in any way. But vampires were odd sometimes. I knew enough to know that elven blood, even diluted, was tempting for vamps due to the power in it. It was why Maria had been so quick to agree to exchange protection from the rest of the coterie for blood, an arrangement that gave her and only her access to mine. The question was whether she'd take issue if I saw Cade again. Or more than one more again.

You don't owe her, or anyone else, anything. The stubborn thought rang in my head as I got into the shower, feeling hollow as the faces of all the people I technically did owe shit to flowed through my mind. Too many obligations, most or all of them to people who wouldn't give a shit if I turned up dead in a vampire's lair beyond the inconvenience it caused their immediate plans. Some would say I deserved it or that they weren't surprised a low-blood would be some kind of vampire-fucking degenerate.

That burned more than the scalding hot water. But why should I let assholes dictate where I found pleasure?

Fuck them. I'm going back.

Not tonight though. I needed distance. A cool head. Cade had pulled a depth of desire from me that I hadn't known existed, like water from a well I'd thought long dry. I'd shut myself down, told myself to focus on my work, because the one and only time I'd tried to claim something good for myself it had gotten me exiled.

That thought circled my brain as I got out of the shower, dressed, and settled at the table to maintain all my weapons. It'd been about a year since The Incident, as it was referred to in my mother's House. I tried pushing the memories away, but they sat there, stubborn and digging in painfully, as though my mind was asking whether I really wanted to take another chance at anything other than being what others wanted me to be.

It'd been late summer. Lyon, France. My home or the nearest big city to it. I was finishing up my annual visit from London when I met someone. Henri was prince of a junior House in the triad making up Lyon's ruling Conclave. He was second-born to a sister who was heir-apparent, weaker in magic than most high-blood elves, and reckless with lack of responsibility or prospects.

I was smitten.

To everyone's surprise, the feeling was mutual.

In the end, the crime of our being together was laid on me, the low-blood born to a shamed mother who'd turned her back on responsibilities to her family and House and married a human. It wasn't forbidden for elves to marry humans, and it happened often enough that there were plenty of us first-generation low-bloods, as the full elves insisted on calling us. But when your mother was a fallen royal, and you were caught in the bed of a prince determined to fuck his way to a similar fall…yeah.

Elves lived long lives and hated to see history repeat itself.

So I was punished. Severely. Only my mother's former status and the fact that I was unusually strong with magic for a half-elf saved me from having a convenient accident for daring to "look above my station."

My mother. My father. Henri. All stood up in front of the Lyon Conclave of Queens as the tribunal judged me and sentenced me to exile.

None of them said anything.

My mother's face was blank but for the tears running down it. She wouldn't do anything to jeopardize my father, who'd be open to reprisals from the elves for knowing too much if she too was sent away. My father kept his mouth shut as well, knowing he was only a mundane guest in a world of magic far beyond his capability to act in.

And Henri? He stood there with the bruises and stiff posture that said he'd taken his punishment already, staring at the floor, all of his many and repeated protestations of love now silent.

It was the first time I'd really, really understood that nobody would be there for me and that it wasn't because I was any kind of bad person or bad at my job.

It was because of shit I'd been born with.

I'd accepted the terms. What else was I supposed to do? Exile to North Carolina was better than death. I could still practice my trade and be a bounty hunter, if under different terms and for much less pay. I could still build a life for myself, if one that was disgraced.

I just couldn't have what I wanted. Or *who* I wanted.

Unless I put up both middle fingers and said "fuck you" to all of them.

To do that, I'd need allies. My thoughts from yesterday came back to me in a rush. Nothing said I had to fall in love with Cade. I didn't have to repeat past mistakes.

But he'd been taken enough with me to ask if I was coming back.

I wasn't too proud to use that to my advantage. Why not make deals with both Maria and him? Confidence returned, and I smiled as I refocused on finishing with my weapons.

I'd figure something out. I always did, even if this time I'd have to go bigger.

Chapter 5: Cade

Cade had to see her again, whatever it took. Even if his own past had taught him trust could be fatal.

He wasn't used to being taken by a fancy like this, and at first, it irritated him. She'd left so easily. Taken everything he had to give all night, poured it straight back, and then just…left.

Sure, she'd looked like she was going to stay, if only for a moment. He'd smelled the desire on her, even over the scents of their overnight activities. But she had to have known that'd mean a breakfast and then bed situation.

Biting was one of her lines. She'd stuck to it and left.

He had to give her credit. First, for following through on her boldness, with no shame and just enough fear to tell him she wasn't brainless. He'd even tried scaring her off, a little frightened himself at how much he wanted to claim her. She'd wrestled with her fear, conquered it, and then…conquered him.

There was no other word for it. He might have been the one holding her down, but he'd taken his cues from her.

It scared him enough that he shifted uneasily against pillows that still smelled like her hair. He'd been conquered once before, far from pleasurably, and it'd resulted in two hundred years of torture.

But Lya wasn't a master vampire. She was a tantalizing rogue of a half-elf who pushed all his buttons simply by existing.

What would it be like now that he had a better idea of how she'd react?

The fire of a challenge sparked in him.

He'd see her again. He'd make sure of it. He just had to figure out who the fuck she was first. Lya the elf-blooded, who practiced martial arts and enchanted him like a succubus even without using Aether on him.

But Lya Who?

No. He wasn't some kind of crazed stalker. Cade knew the difference between a fun hunt and a threatening one, and he wouldn't do anything to make Lya fear him.

Even if part of him, the low, reptilian-brained part amplified by the vampire virus, wanted nothing more than to find her, catch her, and feed from her while he took his pleasure.

No, he told himself more firmly.

Every being had urges, and every being was responsible for controlling those urges where they'd cause harm to another. His old master might have been a depraved monster, but Cade wasn't—not these days, at least—even in search of power and whatever else Lya had sparked in him. He couldn't help drinking from humans; he'd die without it. But there were rules around drinking from Othersiders for very good reasons, reasons he'd learned a hard lesson testing. Lya knew what he was. Human-blooded or not, they'd engaged as Othersiders, and she'd stated her boundaries.

Glamouring her without consent wouldn't be like glamouring a human to survive or maintain the Détente. It'd be magical trespass. Aside from being utterly wrong, it might get him beheaded and burned to ash.

That didn't stop his brain from straying to the thought of her writhing in pleasure beneath him, a deeper pleasure than even sex, brought on first by glamour then by a bite. The herby flavor of elven blood spurting into his mouth as he—

39

Stop it.

Okay, so he had an obsession. It'd been years since he'd had to deal with one of those. There was nothing new under the sun or the moon, and after almost five hundred years, he'd resigned himself to the idea that living apart from a coterie and traveling as a vagabond might be the only way he'd keep himself safe and life interesting. That and a vagabond had independent status. He owed fealty to no one. That he was protected by no one was fine by him. He was old enough to take care of himself and safer for it, even if the itch for more power and security had started again.

Besides, he'd learned the hard way that trust and connections were dangerous. They hurt. They got people killed—and had earned him his first death, an experience he wasn't keen to repeat. Even when they didn't permanently kill, they got everything stripped away, as he'd learned in later events.

Reminding himself of that didn't stop him from wanting Lya more than he'd wanted anyone in his long life.

A knock at the main door to the VIP room shook him from his thoughts. "Sir?"

With a sigh, Cade dragged himself out of bed and answered it, not bothering to dress. "Sorry, I know the time's up. Give me a few minutes please."

"Of course, sir. Will you be needing a to-go meal?"

"Yes. That'd be most accommodating, thank you."

It'd be an extra charge, but he'd accumulated more money over the years than he knew what to do with. Another benefit of being a vagabond—no tithing portions of his income to a Master or Mistress of the City. It'd also be better than having to heat one of the bags of blood he kept in a locked refrigerator in his walk-in closet.

"Of course, sir." The much younger vampire inclined his head and hurried away.

Cade dressed quickly, not wanting to overstay his welcome and risk not being allowed back. Maria was delightfully flexible on arrangements, but she had a nasty temper when someone overstepped. He reckoned he could best her in a dominance battle, but he had no interest in becoming Torsten's number three for the obligatory five-year minimum period if he won or in dealing with the retribution of Maria's rabidly loyal fledgling.

That meant being a good guest while in the Viking's territory.

When he was reasonably clothed, his shirt mostly buttoned, waistcoat hanging open, and jacket slung over his arm, he took one last deep inhale, ensuring he had every nuance of Lya's scent stored in his brain.

If she'd come to Raleigh once, she might again. He wouldn't go out of his way to stalk her, but he wasn't above trying to bump into her.

A pale, blond human woman, wearing the comfortable clothes and eager smile of a blood pet or a junkie, was waiting at the bar when Cade made his way downstairs.

"Good morning, sir," she said in a tone breathy with excitement.

"Good morning, lovely." He offered a small smile as he approached. "Might I take the edge off for you?"

She perked up. "Yes, please."

A junkie then, willing to risk a host losing control and killing her to chase the high of a glamour. Cade didn't feel great about drinking from them, but it'd be rude to turn her down now and he was famished.

Tilting her head up with gentle fingers, he locked eyes with her and loosened the control he maintained over his magic. Glamour spilled free, riding their connection and settling over the woman like a warm blanket.

She swayed, lips parting as her pupils dilated.

Cade took her in his arms before she could fall and bent to her neck. Made the quick bite over the carotid artery that would spill blood into his mouth. Drank.

The edge of exhaustion from the night before faded with each swallow. Warmth spread through him, cutting through the graveyard chill that seeped in if a vampire went too long between feedings or had been more energetic than usual. The stiffness in his muscles and joints eased, which would let him look human when he walked out rather than like a windup toy that was on the verge of needing a crank.

When her heart started pumping faster, he stopped suckling from her and pressed his tongue to the wound. In seconds, a blend of saliva and magic closed the twin punctures, leaving her with just the faintest beginnings of a hickey. A small courtesy but one he always extended, even to junkies and pets who knew what the vampires drinking from them were. They might be completely cared for by their hosts or the coterie, but they still had lives, or might do. He didn't want this one stuck waiting for his bite to heal if she had somewhere to be.

She swayed when he pulled away.

"Easy." Scooping her up, he carried her over to one of the couches and laid her down, feet propped up on the arm. It'd take a while for her to come out of the glamour, but he wasn't just going to leave her on the floor.

When he turned to ask the bartender for a beverage to leave next to her, he found the man already on his way over with a glass of orange juice and a small plate of cookies, a strange look on his face.

"What's wrong?" Cade asked.

"Nothing, sir. You're just...more thoughtful than most of our guests."

Cade studied him. He still smelled almost human, so while he was one of the *moroi*, he was a brand-new one. New vampires had four origins: favored pets, convenient accidents, planned hunts, or attacks by rakshasa too lost to remember the rules. He wouldn't be this calm with a vampire Cade's age if he'd been through one of the latter three experiences. Cade knew that from his own turning.

"You used to be a pet?" Cade asked.

The man nodded. "There was...an incident." He shrugged. "So, here I am. But hey, at least they turned me."

"Indeed." It wasn't guaranteed. If he hadn't been someone's favorite, this handsome bartender would have just been dead. "Am I permitted back, then?"

"Yeah. Philip said that as long as you stay right with Maria, the girl from last night walked out, and you minded your manners, you could keep coming back."

"Appreciated. What was your name?"

"I'm Ricardo. Late night to dawn shift, usually."

That made sense. The newer ones would be put in the riskier daylight positions while they were young enough not to be too bothered by the sun and not too valuable to the coterie just yet.

"Good to meet you, Ricardo." Cade shook his hand. "Until next time."

"Next time, sir."

Cade picked up Lya's scent again at the lift, shuddering as it enveloped him in the enclosed space. The blood he'd just taken decided to concentrate itself in his crotch, of course, and he had to leave the elevator with his jacket held over his front to avoid looking like some kind of pervert.

As he stepped outside, he was distracted again by Lya's fading scent. It stopped at the curb with no spike of fear, so at least she'd gotten to the car safely.

He frowned, annoyed all over again as he realized he was more worried about her than he was about getting home. That was the problem with the shorter nights of summer—getting home when he'd indulged himself and overslept.

Idiot. So taken by a woman that you're taking risks with daylight.

The entry of the building was north-facing, still in shadow with the sun barely up. He wouldn't burst into flame or anything as dramatic as the human films suggested, and he could walk for short distances at full noon without any effects worse than a bad sunburn. But he hated sunburns, and he hated the itching that lasted for days after even a brief exposure to the sun.

Nothing for it. Fortunately, he lived nearby, on the second floor of a modern building in an interior and north-facing apartment that never quite got full sun, especially when he pulled the blackout curtains.

He'd just gotten in the door and locked it behind him when his cell phone rang. Tired all over again and itchy from sun exposure, he ignored it and headed for the bathroom and a cold shower. He was smoothing aloe vera over his face when the damned device went off again.

The only people who had the number were vampires. If they were calling multiple times after sunup, it had to be important.

With a sigh, Cade checked the caller ID.

Maria.

He winced, wondering what he'd done to draw her attention. Torsten might be Master in Raleigh, and Aron might carry out his wishes, but anyone with a brain knew that Maria was the driving force behind the coterie's success, even if Torsten and Aron refused to acknowledge it.

"Maria." He kept his voice light but didn't bother trying to hide his tiredness. "To what do I owe the late call?"

"Long night, muffin?"

"You could say that. The hospitality at your new club leaves nothing to be desired."

"So I hear. I also hear that you've met the lovely Mademoiselle Lydia of House Desmarais."

Cade froze. He didn't buy the teasing note in Maria's voice. He'd heard it before, when she was setting someone up for a verbal skewering.

"Half-elf?" she prompted. "Entertainingly bold?"

"We got acquainted," he said carefully, not daring to lie and not wanting to give away that he hadn't had a surname or even a full first name, apparently. "I wasn't aware you had an interest."

"Oh I do. I very much do."

Swallowing a burst of panic that seemed to curdle the blood he'd just taken, Cade leaned on the counter. He should have guessed that a prize like Lya wouldn't just wander in off the street with no strings attached.

"May I ask the nature of the interest?" he said. *Please don't say she's your lover.*

"Hmm."

Cade let the silence hang, suspecting it was equal parts Maria thinking through the angles and her playing a game.

"I suppose you may, in exchange for telling me *your* interest," she finally said.

"I can't just enjoy a drink with a beautiful woman?"

"As long as you're both drinking booze and she stays ass above grass, I don't give a damn what you do with her."

"So it's a blood donation?"

"Yes. Every six weeks, in exchange for free passage in Raleigh."

That explained at least some of Lya's no biting line and was somewhat a relief, even if it made jealousy spark. He tamped it down. No vampire could afford to act on the emotion. He thought it was bullshit that Lya would have to pay for passage with blood, since any Othersider who wasn't full-blooded could

45

technically pass through as the mundanes did, but he supposed it bought her a measure of protection.

Ah. Hence the call. Lya had mentioned having friends in town, and given Maria's ambitions, he suspected protection wasn't the only reason for this conversation. But he was smart enough not to mention that.

"I see," Cade said. "Well. I can assure you no blood was exchanged on either side and I have no intention of harming her."

"See that it stays that way." Maria had dropped the flirty tones and was all business now. "Because, Cade, darling? You may have the privileges of a vagabond, but everyone wears out their welcome eventually."

"Is that a threat?" Shock made him reply far more coldly than was polite. As long as they didn't break any laws of either Otherside or the mundanes, vagabonds were permitted to come and go unharassed and were owed a certain level of guest courtesy.

"I wouldn't dare. I'm just letting you know where we stand. Lya bought protection as well as passage," Maria said far too lightly, confirming his earlier inference. "If I hear that she's been hurt, you and I are going to have a problem."

"I appreciate that." He bit his tongue before he could say he wasn't hunting her. It'd be a lie because, while he wasn't *actively* pursuing the woman, he fully intended to taste more than her pussy. Assuming she'd let him, of course. "In the interest of avoiding problems, I'll be by soon to discuss renewing my guest privileges."

"I see. I suppose it has been six months already." The line went silent as she considered that, even if she had no say in the matter. "Fine. Good talk, sweets. Be good. Bye now."

Maria ended the call, leaving Cade just a shade shy of furious.

It had been a long time since someone tried to warn him off like that. Well intended or not, the only person whose opinion mattered in all of this was Lya's.

Assuming he could find her again, of course.

Chapter 6: Lya

I knocked on the water-stained door of apartment 302, hoping this summons would go better than the first one I'd delivered this afternoon. An argument going on inside got louder before a man whose alcohol-ravaged face matched my file cracked it.

"Yeah? Who're you?" he said.

"Anthony Buncombe?" I held out the folded papers. "You've been served."

Anthony tried to shut the door on me, but I blocked it with my foot just long enough to get the summons in the door.

It slammed with the paperwork on the right side, and I hustled my way back downstairs. The guy was just a mundane, but the lead-alloy bullets in most guns would kill me just as dead as a human if he decided to shoot the messenger. Weres and vamps would heal up before they could die, but not me or anyone else with elf blood. The lead in them poisoned us, fast. I'd never been shot, and I wasn't keen to start with it today.

Fortunately, today was not that day, and serving that summons was the last thing on my to-do list. It was Saturday, which meant I only worked the afternoon, another lucky break. Me turning up late after last night's events would have been the excuse Farand was looking for to treat me even shittier than usual. Maybe to say that I was in breach of the terms of my exile and finally have an excuse to mete out a punishment of his own.

For once though, I didn't let myself be bothered by it. I was making a plan for myself, one that featured a future sans-Farand. The more I thought about it, the more defiant I felt. If nobody wanted me here, why should I stay?

The terms of my exile were bollocks. No laws had been broken. I'd just gotten "above myself" as far as the queens were concerned.

Stop thinking about that. What you focus on expands.

I walked back to the bail bond office to do the paperwork that'd wrap up my day, thinking hard on where I wanted to go with my life. It was difficult though because, at the moment, the only place I wanted to go was back to Raleigh. Back to a certain tall, dark, and handsome vampire.

I didn't believe in fated mates or twin flames, and I was smart enough to know he had to be playing a long game for my blood. But I couldn't stop thinking about the thrill of ordering him around. He was far more powerful than me, but for now, his plans served me and my pleasure like nobody else ever had.

As much as I tried to focus on my paperwork, my mind kept wandering. What would it be like to let him take the dominant role?

Just go back to Raleigh.

After catching myself reading the same line for the ninth time, I decided to call it a day. None of this needed to be done today. I was just doing my usual fear-driven overperformance bullshit. As though getting paperwork done faster was what would get Farand to back off or treat me fairly. His bigotry was just that, and all it had to do with paperwork was as an excuse to give me more of it.

Disgusted with myself, I filed what I'd managed to complete, locked up my computer, and headed out. The whole drive home, I tried to talk myself out of going back to Raleigh.

Vampire help never came cheap and often came bloody, one way or another. Maria offered protection and Cade was a hell of a lay, but they'd both have their own agendas. Convincing either of them to help me with mine would probably cost more than I was willing to pay.

There had to be another way that I could outmaneuver Farand and the queens of the Lyon Conclave.

What if I just left town? Except no, the terms were clear on that one: leave town and I'd be the bounty. Elven society was as much about appearances as reality, and I had to be *seen* to be controlled and humiliated if I was going to serve as the proper lesson for others.

Shame blended with fury and burned in my gut. I was worth so much more than this. I just couldn't see a way out yet, beyond my plan to use my vampire connections.

That didn't feel right either though.

Someone with my skills should be able to make their own way. Just because my cousins were determined to piss on me didn't mean I had to make myself small enough to fit under the spray.

My phone rang as I pulled up to my apartment. It was Shonda, a human woman I'd met shortly after arriving. We had an on-again, off-again acquaintance, but we always had a good time when we went out. I answered as I got out of the car, hoping this would precipitate something suitably distracting, even if it meant a night tamping down on my magic and pretending to be human.

"Hey Shonda, how's things?" I said.

"Hey girl! Everything's good, you?"

"Can't complain." Even though I really, really could. I just didn't know Shonda like that. I injected a note of enthusiasm and interest into my voice as I unlocked my front door, hurried in, and locked it behind me, raising my voice to be heard over the tinkling bells. "What's up?"

"Girls' night. Friend of a friend got dumped and wants to do a thing. Vibe seems like your kind of people and your kind of night. You in?"

I wondered what my kind of people entailed but fuck it. I hadn't done a girls' night in ages. "Hell yeah, when and where?"

"We've got table reservations for nine, new place in Raleigh. Nightshade."

The club I'd been at last night. Un-fucking-believable. I hesitated.

"Lya? Sorry, I know it's last-minute, I just thought—"

"No, no! It's great. I was just trying to remember if I had anything I needed not to be hungover for tomorrow, but I'm good. I'll see you there at nine. Thanks for the invite!"

"Yay! See ya, girl."

I hung up and threw my phone in the general direction of the couch.

It's fine. What are the odds Cade will be there two nights in a row?

***

Cade was there two nights in a row.

I glanced at the booth where he'd been the night before as I trailed in at the back of the group of women, some of whom had already been pregaming from the scent of rosé clinging to them.

As though the vampire could sense me, his head snapped around from where he idly watched a group of humans like a lion wondering if zebras were worth the bother. His lips parted slightly in disbelief, and those nearly black eyes of his bored into me. At the memory of them looking down at me from much closer, my core clenched, and I swallowed hard, self-consciously smoothing the dress I'd thrown on in an effort to fit in with what I'd correctly assumed Shonda's office friends would be wearing.

"Come on, Lya!" Shonda said. "The table's this way."

Shaking off the effect of Cade's gaze, I slapped on a smile and followed them. There was no way my luck was good enough that I'd meet someone who made my head spin without a glamour, could offer the out I wanted if I was brave enough to pay the price for it, and then happened to be around two nights running.

Some people would call it a sign, but I didn't trust it. At all. I'd trusted in the Universe and Fate and all that bullshit once before and it had gotten me here.

Not again.

As Shonda went to the bar for a round, I shook off my funk and did my best to make small talk with some of the others in the group. Connections made the world go round, and I wasn't above making them with mundanes.

"So Shonda says you're a bail bond runner? What exactly does that mean?" asked a brunette named Kerry.

"Basically a bounty hunter, but you can't call it that in North Carolina."

That drew gasps and looks of interest.

"Oh my gawd, that sounds so much more interesting than marketing. Do you, like, get to shoot people?"

I forced a smile and recited my usual line. "I do my best not to. Hard to collect bail money then."

"Damn, girl, you're a badass! Can you go scare Steve or something?"

"Ha. I would, if it wouldn't get my license taken away. If he owed child support or something though, I can't say I'd turn down a job to say hello." I gave them a wicked smile, which titillated them and set them laughing with just a hint of vengeance behind their glee.

With some urging, I trotted out one of my safer mundane stories before turning the conversation back toward Nicole, the woman we were here to commiserate with. Her brown eyes were reddened like she'd been crying, although she was putting on a defiant face—the one some women wore when they were determined to prove they didn't need any man and especially not the one they'd caught cheating.

I felt for her. I hadn't caught Henri with someone else, but I did feel betrayed.

I pushed the memory aside, determined to make the most of a rare invite out. I also did my best to avoid looking in the direction of Cade's table again, although the other women had no such compunction.

"Y'all see that guy in the booth? Other side of the room? Three-piece suit, nice hair. What's he doing alone? I would eat him alive."

Literally would be the other way round.

"He looks like he'd enjoy that. Grr."

Actually, he does enjoy a good attempt at it.

Fortunately, Shonda's return with a tray full of shots interrupted the increasingly creative speculations of what Cade might enjoy in bed. Philip was behind her with a second fully laden tray of cocktails, which he deposited with a small flourish and a coy smile.

"Your food will be out shortly, ladies. If I can do anything else to make your night more pleasant, please don't hesitate to let me know." The vampire carefully ignored me.

He was out of human hearing range—but not vampire—when Nicole roused herself and said, "He can bend me over that bar is what he can do. Yummy."

I caught the missed step that told me Philip had heard, but he kept walking as the other women cackled and raised shots.

I made myself smile and raised mine, singing out a "Cheers!" along with them before downing it. Tequila. Someone was looking to get sloppy drunk tonight, and for once, I blessed my hyperactive metabolism. I skipped the salt and lime, earning me immediate cheers and howls from the rest.

Okay, maybe Shonda was right. Maybe these were my kind of people, even if they weren't Othersiders or bounty hunters.

What could it hurt to ease up a little and have fun with them?

I let Nicole and Shonda drag me out to the dance floor, despite their teasing about keeping my purse. I wasn't going to leave weapons unattended in this group. It didn't take much coaxing for me to get going, especially when they switched from generic electronica to my favorite 90s' jams. I ignored the weight of Cade's gaze on me and lost myself to the music, remembering better days until the scent of food brought me out of my nostalgia-fueled trance at the prospect of whatever Shonda had ordered for the table.

"Girl," she said as I slid onto the curved booth bench wrapping around the table. "You need to go hook you that man."

I stuffed my face with a slider and groaned with pleasure at the taste of quality beef and fancy cheese. "What—oh. Him."

"Yes. *Him.*"

Cade was watching us again. When I risked a look into his eyes, he toasted me with what I suspected was an untouched whiskey neat.

The other women immediately fell on me.

"Ohmigod, girl, get some."

"Go see if he has friends."

"Wait! We need to go to the powder room first."

Blinking at the onslaught, I snagged a slider in each hand as Shonda and another woman whose name I'd missed hustled me up and to the restroom.

Cade watched, amused, and I narrowed my eyes at him in warning before pointedly stuffing the sliders in my face in a very unladylike fashion. Yeah, I wanted him again. But the more the possibility of a second night built, the more anxious I got. I couldn't even say why, other than a sense of inevitability that set goosebumps rippling over my skin, despite the warmth in the room.

He just smiled as we passed, like he was glad I was eating to keep up my strength.

I humored the other women when we got in front of the mirrors, adjusting my bra and twining a few curls around my fingers while they fixed makeup and pumped each other up.

This wasn't how I usually did things, at all, but...fuck it.

When we re-emerged onto the dance floor, Cade was gone from his booth. My hunter's senses told me he was somewhere behind me, likely at the bar, but I didn't turn around. There was no use looking for him in the crush of people, although my new acquaintances tried.

"Let's just dance," I said. "Life's too short to wait on one man."

"I couldn't agree more." Cade's voice in my ear from behind me made me jump and whirl a little too quickly for human, and the other women shrieked excitedly. The vampire leaned back gracefully, avoiding spilling the trio of drinks he carried before sidling around to offer them to the three of us. "Philip told me you were drinking Long Islands. Can I offer a refill?"

With broad smiles and heart eyes, the other two women accepted theirs.

I made a point of looking Cade in the eye as I took mine. "Smooth."

He grinned, carefully hiding his fangs with his lower lip. "I try."

"They want men, not drinks."

"Not *just* men. Dance with me?"

I shook my head, but it was resignation, not refusal.

Of course, the DJ chose that moment to play "Peaches & Cream," which I—and half the bar, from the screams—found irresistible. Suddenly, everyone on the floor was coupled.

Keeping my drink steady, I spun to put my back to Cade's front and moved sinuously against him, the echo of last night kickstarting my libido since I already knew where this could go.

"I didn't expect to see you back again so soon." Cade's voice in my ear was already as tight as his trousers must've been, from the way he felt pressing against me.

"I didn't plan to come back so soon."

"You didn't have fun last night?"

"Oh, I did, but that kind of fun gets women like me in trouble."

"And what kind of woman are you, Lya?"

I arched back and nipped his earlobe, unable to help myself, thrilled by his sharp inhale. "The kind who has made too many bad decisions in the past."

He didn't answer for a minute. Then with a smooth twirl, he spun me to face him, tugging me close to grind our hips together.

I groaned, equally for that as for "Thong Song" coming on next. "Did you give the DJ a 'fuck Lya' playlist?"

Cade chuckled. "No, but if these are the magic words, I'll go tell him to play more like this."

"Bastard." I couldn't put any bite behind the words because, despite my earlier reluctance to put myself in his arms again, here I was, and here I wanted to be. "Cade…"

He shivered under my hand. "Careful. You don't need magic to put a spell on me."

A slow song came on, and he freed me when I tensed at the prospect of something more intimate.

"Enjoy your night, Lya," he said. "If you're looking for an afterparty, wink on your way out the door and head for East Davie Street. I'll catch you up."

I took myself and my Long Island Iced Tea back to the table, feeling conflicted all over again because I shouldn't want him this much. I couldn't afford it. But I very much wanted a repeat of last night, if only to claw a little fun out of my time in the Triangle when everyone wanted me beat down and sad.

And if he was this taken with me, I wanted a shot to win over a potential business partner.

That meant playing a little dangerously.

Chapter 7: Cade

Cade forced himself not to watch Lya the rest of the night, determined not to be *that* creep. She was already skittish, for reasons he couldn't figure out, given how forward she'd been last night. The human women with her maybe, making her worried about hiding herself as an Othersider? Either way, the moment she'd tensed, he'd known he had to back off. Not for Maria's threat but for Lya's peace of mind. Scaring her now would go against the whole point.

A trio of Torsten's vampires came in, and he raised a hand to signal that they were welcome to join him before they had to wonder about his intentions. Of course, they noticed Lya as quickly as he had both nights. They also dismissed her just as quickly.

"Maria's," Lucien muttered, the single word heavy with regret.

Oscar gave Lya a last evaluating look. "If that's the blood Maria's getting, my bet is she knocks Aron off his pedestal in the next decade. Maybe less."

"That fast?"

The third *moroi*, Rani, nodded. "I believe it."

She glanced at Cade, as though remembering he wasn't one of the coterie and evaluating whether it was safe to speak in front of him.

Cade spotted an opportunity to gather information and offered a lazy half-smile. "I'm just a visitor. Grateful for Maria's hospitality though."

That drew the attention of all three of the others, and Oscar tilted his head. "Don't you mean Torsten's hospitality?"

Aware of the fine line he walked, Cade shrugged. "Of course."

Oscar's sharp look turned sly. Lucien and Rani relaxed.

"Truthfully, I've been impressed with what I've seen of Maria," Cade said genuinely. He didn't appreciate being threatened by her, but he wasn't too proud to admit she was doing an excellent, if undervalued, job here in Raleigh. "I've visited dozens of territories over the years, and the Triangle is one of the most stable, despite the mixed-faction power-sharing agreement. Maria seems forward-thinking in that regard."

"She is," Oscar hastened to assure him. "It's not easy, having a full elven conclave in Chapel Hill and that joined werecat pride up in Durham. Too many predators in the area, and that's not even mentioning that bitch Callista standing over all of us as Arbiter, whatever faction she belongs to. But Maria's made some good decisions since becoming Torsten's third."

And you three are angling for positions of power and influence when she ascends. Noted. Cade smiled. "These venues primary among those decisions, at least for those of us honored to guest here."

The other three grinned back, barely hiding their fangs.

"For those of us who live here as well. On that note, I have a mighty thirst." Rani rose and headed for the dance floor in a whirl of blue skirts that had Cade thinking of Lya, dressed in red and—he glanced at the floor—currently back to dancing.

Don't stare. Mind your business.

And he did, making small talk with whichever of the three other *moroi* were relaxing in the booth over the course of the next two hours.

"You're not hunting tonight?" Oscar asked at one point.

Cade smiled easily. "I fed before coming here."

Which was true—he found it easier to blend in with humans and use less glamour when his skin was warm and he was moving smoothly—just not the whole truth.

He didn't peg Lya for the jealous type, but he found himself not wanting to give her the impression she was anything less than special. It irked him all over again. That wasn't a good long-term survival strategy. But it was how he felt, and he'd learned to listen to those nudges of intuition.

"Fair enough." Oscar's eyes tracked a specific spot on the dance floor. "There goes the half-elf. Damn. It was delicious just watching her."

Cade's gaze snapped to Lya, just in time to see her look their way. Her gaze darted between him and Oscar.

She didn't wink as she followed her friends out the door.

Was it because she didn't want to see him? Or because she recognized Oscar as one of Torsten's *moroi* and didn't want to tip him off?

Oscar clapped him on the shoulder. "I'm off to catch dinner. Stay well, friend."

"And you."

Cade forced himself to wait until Oscar, Rani, and Lucien were all occupied with dancing or quick feeds before leaving.

Unlike this morning, Lya's scent didn't dissipate at the curb, although most of the group's did. Hope quickened in him as he followed it south to East Davie Street. Then to the cozy corner bar across from his lodgings, where a glance in the window showed him Lya, nursing a highball of something dark.

From the way she tensed, she knew the minute he entered the place. Of course she did. Was her spatial awareness because she was a half-elf in dangerous territory or something else?

She toasted him when he edged up to the bar and leaned against it. "Figured you'd find me."

He didn't answer, too overcome by the scent of her, heightened by dancing and her walk here from the club in the humid night. Then she glanced at him, the nervous pinch of her brow breaking the spell.

"You're hard to miss." He resisted the urge to touch her, waiting to see whether it was him making her nervous or something else.

"That why your friends had their eye on me all night?"

Cade grimaced. "They're Maria's."

"You know Maria?" Lya straightened, suddenly much more serious.

"I know her and your arrangement with her."

Lya looked for all the world like a hawk trying to decide whether she'd tackled prey too big to fly off with. "I see."

"Don't worry. I've been duly warned."

She arched an eyebrow. "Yet here you are."

"The warning wasn't about last-night topics," Cade said, voice low. He let his eyes drop to the pulse in her throat.

"Ah. Okay then. Good." She slugged half her drink and started jittering her leg.

The bartender wandered over then away again to ring the last-call bell when Cade shook his head.

"Hey," he said, suddenly uncertain of how fast he could move in his pursuit of her blood. "If you don't want anything more—"

"Shut up. You promised me an afterparty."

Anticipation and pleasure hit him so hard he shuddered. "I did indeed. Shall we?"

Lya rose without finishing the drink, digging in her purse.

"Let me." He fished out his wallet and flashed a twenty, his smallest bill. "Will that cover it?"

"More than."

"Good. I'd like them to remember you fondly. Just in case you come back."

Her laugh made him feel light and daring, like he had in his past life and less frequently the older he got. Life was a sunk cost at this point. He was invested in hanging on to it because of what he'd had to do to break free of his master and surviving what had come after, doubly so because he'd already seen five centuries.

Lya gave breath to the embers again and maybe, just maybe, made it about more than gaining enough power to stay alive.

She frowned when he walked her across the road and keyed them into the apartment building. "Here? Really?"

"What, were you expecting some kind of—"

"Something more stereotypical, to be sure."

"Nothing typical about a vagabond's life."

"Ah. That explains it."

Cade glanced at her but couldn't read her expression. "Explains?"

"Why you don't seem worried about Maria."

He snorted and led her to the stairs. Lya wore heels, but one floor should be fine. "Trust me, I have a healthy respect for her. I'm simply not beholden to her."

"Hm. Interesting."

That was encouraging.

Tense with unusual nervousness, Cade led her to his front door. He hadn't had anyone here since he'd moved in a year and a half ago. The risk was too great. But he hoped, in reciprocating the risk she'd taken in being vulnerable with him last night, that she'd take him seriously and not as some sleazy one- or two-night stand.

That idea—that this might be more than just sex or even blood—agitated him enough that his heart beat almost human fast, but he couldn't shake it.

He had to win her over, even if only to figure out how to end his fascination with her.

"Damn," Lya said admiringly when she was inside and he'd flicked the lights on. Chrome appliances, marble countertops, and hardwood floors shone, all the more for the closed blackout curtains. "Vagabonds can afford this?"

"I can." He smiled, pleased by her reaction. "Make yourself comfortable. Do you want a drink?"

"Just some water." She looked him up and down then set her purse on the counter, checking it for something. "Need to stay hydrated."

"I'd recommend it, if you're up for round...what'd we get to last night?"

"I lost track."

As he passed Lya to get a glass, she grabbed him and pushed him backward aggressively.

Cade's reflexes kicked in as his back hit the refrigerator. His fingers tangled in her hair and pulled her head back to bare her throat as his other arm wrapped around her waist and pulled her flush against him. An intoxicating blend of fear and arousal spiked from her as her pupils dilated and her pulse jumped in her neck.

"That's how half-elves get themselves bitten by anyone with less self-control," he warned her when he'd caught his breath.

"Just needed to be sure you'd still play by the rules, now that we're on your turf." Her hard-edged smile said she'd been testing him again—as did the small silver knife she tapped against his flank, one he hadn't noticed until just then. She could have gutted him even as he bit her.

Arousal hit him fast and hard.

Here was a woman he could respect. She wasn't just food or a fuck but a challenge. Maybe even an equal, even if she was human-blooded. Pulling that trick on a vampire his age in his own nest just to test him? Unbelievably ballsy.

He did what he'd been dying to do all night: kissed her. Claimed her mouth, roughly and completely as her arms twined up and around his neck. The cold flat of the blade against his spine was ample reminder of what would happen if he didn't follow the rules, but he wished she'd slip with her tongue.

"Forget the water," she said when she pulled away. "I want you. Now."

Cade inhaled deeply. She didn't smell or sound intoxicated, and her pupils were responding normally. She'd been steady enough not to nick him while they kissed. If now was what she wanted, now was what she'd have.

He spun her to face the kitchen counter and bent her over it with a hand between her shoulder blades.

The knife clattered to the counter.

She made a soft noise of surprise and arousal before he pulled up the hem of her dress and leaned hard against her ass, blanketing her with his body.

"Like this?" he growled.

"Yes. Goddess yes."

The heels she still wore brought her to the perfect height.

Cade tugged her thong from her hips and skimmed his fingers between her legs to find her already plenty wet. "Condom?"

"Yes. Now." She pushed back against him, her voice breathy and her skin hot.

"At your service." He opened his trousers just enough to get his already throbbingly hard cock out, dug one of the condoms he'd bought earlier out of his wallet, and rolled it on. Her pants of anticipation drove him to go faster, but he forced himself to go slow as he pressed into her.

Heat enveloped him as she moaned then pushed back against him, swiveling her hips like she did on the dance floor.

Fucking her had been incredible last night. It was better now, with her scent filling his nest, the animalistic pleasure of bending her over the kitchen counter he'd never used and rocking deeply into her with every thrust.

Don't bite her don't bite her don't bite her.

The thought echoed in his head, the only thing keeping him focused on her body long enough to bring her first. He kept his hand firmly between her shoulder blades, no matter how she writhed, gripping her hip with his other hand to keep her steady. He'd give her pleasure, but he'd take his at the same time, and right now, it pleased him to remind her that he would be in charge any time he wanted to be, little silver knives or not.

When she cried out his name and tightened around him, Cade buried his face in the curve of her shoulder, trying to be satisfied with taking in her smell rather than her blood as he gritted his teeth and followed her.

They stood there, panting, until he had the presence of mind to pull himself together.

After a quick kiss to the nape of her neck, he pulled away and discarded the condom before gathering her to him. "All good?"

"So good." The way her head lolled back against his shoulder had him checking for signs of intoxication again.

"You sure you're okay?"

"Oh fuck yeah. Unless you can be drunk on sex." She stiffened. "Oh Goddess, that was awful."

With a relieved chuckle, Cade scooped her up and headed for the bedroom. "As long as you remember this and feel good about it whenever you decide to leave."

"That's almost what I'm afraid of." Her voice had gone quiet and small.

Laying her on the bed, he crouched and caressed her cheek. "Oh? Why's that, beautiful?"

"I can't afford feeling good or happy."

The way she flinched and curled up then, as though to protect herself, broke something in him unexpectedly. Lya looked to be in her thirties. What had already happened to her to make her feel that way?

"Hey." He waited until she looked at him. "You okay? Do you want me to call you a cab?"

She studied him for so long he was afraid he'd done something wrong, that the answer might be yes. Then she extended a hand. "I want you to hold me, and then I want to fuck you until I can't."

A wave of emotion passed over him. Something that felt like equal parts lust and triumph. To hide it, he knelt and slipped her heels off then eased onto the bed behind her, pulling her against him. "Whatever you need, I can give you."

Lya shivered in his arms. "Don't make promises you can't keep."

"I don't." He fully intended to give her whatever it took, if it brought her to him.

She twisted to look at him, the depths of her eyes haunted. Started to speak. Swallowed the words and kissed him instead.

"If nothing else, you make me believe it." She pushed him onto his back and straddled him, resting her forehead against his, then planted little kisses all over his face and neck. He almost missed her whisper. "I need to believe you, Cade."

He didn't know what she was running from, and he didn't care.

What had started as a hunt for powerful blood was passing through the sexual and turning into something emotional at a dizzyingly fast pace. He couldn't even say why. Only that he felt fiercely protective—and fiercely aroused by the fact that this woman, whoever she was, seemed inclined to trust him when he could have her powerless and drained whenever he wanted.

It wasn't the needy faith of a junkie either. It was something more courageous and vulnerable, and he wanted more of it.

No. He wanted *all* of it and all of her.

Cade rolled her onto her back and gripped her chin, enjoying her little gasp and the dilation of her pupils. "Believe me."

He lowered his mouth to hers to devour her in a way she'd permit, hoping to distract her with the promise of more orgasms until he could figure out what she really needed. Until then, he'd just have to live with the idea that this was all she wanted from him, even if that idea was starting to hurt in a way he told himself it shouldn't.

Chapter 8: Lya

I nearly groaned when I woke to the scent of Cade's sheets and our wild evening. I'd spent the night. Again. This time it was at his place, his arm curled around my waist and his face tucked lightly between my shoulder blades, right where his hand had pressed heavy the night before.

Why the fuck did I keep falling asleep in strange beds, with him of all people? He could wake up and decide to eat me, and regardless of my show with the knife last night, there wouldn't be much I could do about it.

As I tried to figure out whether I had a death wish and how to extricate myself without waking the vampire, he mumbled, "Morning. I think."

The way his cool breath tickled against my spine made me shiver.

Maybe going for flippant would make this whole thing less awkward. "You think? Don't you have some kind of, I dunno, internal clock? Seems like a safety measure."

"Don't you have some kind of sense of survival that would keep you awake after fucking a vampire? This is the second time you've fallen asleep in my bed. I almost think you like me."

I flushed, glad he couldn't see my face. I deserved that, but it made me cranky. With a huff, I tried to shove his arm off me.

Didn't work. I didn't budge him a centimeter.

Cade chuckled, sending goosebumps over me. "Come on. Have a lie-in. This is nice."

"What is? A chance at breakfast in bed?"

"You said it, not me. But no."

"What then?" I held off asking as long as I could, but he had my curiosity hooked.

His body curled tighter against mine, and his voice sent a flutter through me as he murmured in my ear. "Waking up next to someone warm, with a spark of magic in her veins. It feels like cuddling a sunbeam. Here I thought elves were supposed to be beings of shadow."

I wanted to laugh at how cheesy that sounded, but something wouldn't let me. Not when he'd sounded so earnest.

I twisted in his embrace, and he pulled back to blink sleepily at me, long lashes fluttering languidly. He wasn't hunting. Not actively. He was actually kind of cute, with his dark hair all mussed and his fangs back behind his lips.

Oh right. Fangs. He could afford to play the long game.

His brow puckered slightly at my scrutiny. "What?"

"Am I a hunt for you?"

Another long, sleepy blink. "In a way. I'd be a fool to pass up a chance at Otherside blood." At my frown, he offered a cheeky grin wide enough to show his fangs. "Don't worry. You'll beg me for that too."

Jaw dropped, I turned all the way over and stared at him. "You cocky son of a—"

His mouth on mine cut me off, cool lips with just the faintest press of fang behind them. His fingers running down my spine made me arch into him before he splayed his hand and rolled to shift me on top of him.

When he pulled back, the look on his face was no longer innocent. "Even if you didn't want to grace me with your blood,

I'd enjoy this. It's nice, not having to pull a glamour and hide what I am or play bedroom politics with another vampire."

I wanted to be mad at him. But the kiss had left me breathless, and if I was honest with myself, I felt the same way. I couldn't show all of me to a human. The high-bloods were all busy playing their game of Houses, and the other low-bloods were busy trying to marry up. Why not enjoy myself with a vampire?

A flashback from last night hit me. *Whatever you need, I can give you.*

He'd had no idea what he was saying, but he'd given me a spark of hope I clung to desperately.

Could I really accept it? The only way to find out would be to at least try.

I didn't say anything as I slowly lowered myself back down to stretch out on top of him. He made a pleased little sound and tugged the blankets higher to cover my back. It was warm enough in the flat that I didn't need them—vamps seemed to need their environments hot, when they could get away with it—but I appreciated the gesture. Almost like he cared.

He ran his fingers along my spine some more. After a while, I drifted off again, soothed in a way that maybe I shouldn't have been, given he'd admitted he'd be happy to eat me.

"Lya."

I shifted, blinking awake again and frowning when I realized I was still in bed with Cade and not at home. The light at the bottom of the blackout curtains over the bedroom window was much stronger. "Shit. Sorry."

"Don't be. Your phone is ringing." His voice was heavy with languor and sleep. Not surprising, given it had to be close to noon and I'd probably used the extra energy he'd gotten from whoever he'd drunk from last night.

That thought stayed with me as I slipped from the sheets and went to the kitchen to find my purse. He didn't know me from

Lilith, but he'd brought me to his nest and let me fall asleep here. A vampire old enough to be this successful as a vagabond would be strong and hard to kill, but if someone like me was going to have a chance at it, now would be the best one.

Maybe we both made stupid choices with the other. That set a little flutter in my stomach that I recognized and didn't like for the way things had ended up the last time I'd felt it.

I found my phone right before it would have gone to voicemail and answered without checking the caller ID. "Desmarais."

"Where the hell are you?" Farand asked. "I've been trying to reach you all morning."

"I'm out." That came shorter than I'd intended it to, but I was annoyed. I didn't owe him my whereabouts.

"I know that. I sent Pia to pick you up and apparently you're not home."

Pushed into full-on anger, I moved farther from the bedroom and lowered my voice. "I know we have an agreement, but it's my day off, Farand. I—"

"Callista doesn't give a shit for your days off. She wants to see you. Now."

Cold chills raced over me. What the fuck did Callista want with me? The woman effectively acted as a mob boss for the area. It was the only way a power-sharing arrangement between the three major Otherside factions hadn't devolved into territory grabs and retaliatory backstabbing. Nobody knew what she was, but she was stronger than the vampire Master of Raleigh, the triad of queens making up the local conclave, and the leaders of the joined wereleopard and werejaguar pride. Not only was she stronger, but she also had a secretive group of spies called Watchers who kept an eye on things for her.

Watchers who might be tracking me, if Callista wanted to see me. *Shit.* My gut clenched, and I swallowed.

71

"Lydia?"

I forced spit back into my mouth. "Yeah. I'll be there."

"Now."

"I mean, yeah, in forty-five minutes to an hour."

"Where the fuck are you?"

"I'm *busy*, Farand. I was enjoying my *day off* because I didn't expect a summons. I will get there as soon as I can." Although it galled me to say the words, I added, "My apologies for missing your calls."

I was under no obligation to explain myself to him and had nothing to be sorry for, but he was easier to deal with when I pretended to be.

After a silence long enough to make the point that I was on his shitlist, Farand said, "You're on thin ice, Desmarais. Goddess knows nobody will be surprised when you finally fall through. Maybe that day is today." When I didn't answer, he added, "Fine. I will tell Callista she can expect you within the hour. Don't make me play secretary again, or you'll regret it."

The call ended, and I scrubbed a hand over my face, trying to figure out how the hell to play this one. Stopping home to shower and change would add too much time, especially if—as the missed calls on my phone indicated—I'd been expected two hours ago.

"Fuck," I whispered. Nothing for it. I'd have to turn up dressed in last night's club outfit smelling like vampire and sex.

"You can shower before you go. If you have time."

I jumped and whirled, biting back a scream at Cade's voice from the bedroom door. He looked sleepy and pale as he slumped against the doorframe with his hair disturbed by sex and sleep, not the least bit dangerous.

A smile flickered at the corners of his lips. "Sorry. You sounded upset. Anything I can do?"

"The shower would be a huge help, actually. I've, ah, been summoned. My boss has no respect for days off or personal boundaries."

Not a total lie. Callista was Farand's indirect boss, so she was mine too.

"Help yourself to whatever you need." He disappeared back into the bedroom, reappearing with my dress on a hanger and my heels hanging from his fingers.

"Thank you." I exchanged a quick kiss for them as I hurried into the bathroom. Hopefully the steam would get the wrinkles out from it being on the floor all night. I didn't believe in walks of shame, but nobody with sense gave Callista any clues to use as leverage.

Of course, that assumed none of the three vamps who'd been with Cade at the club last night had been Watchers.

No, do not fixate on it. Just get washed up and get out.

Cade was still stark naked when I got out of the bathroom, dressed in yesterday's outfit but at least smelling clean. The dozens of large and small scars I'd noted while exploring his skin the last two nights stood out as paler lines on his lean body, making me wonder who he'd been before he'd been turned. Some of those looked like the clean cuts of a blade, while others looked more like bullet holes. However long ago they'd been made, I suspected they meant he was dangerous in more ways than just his fangs or his glamour or the ridiculous skill with which he made me come.

He caught me staring and lifted an eyebrow. "See something you like?"

"Hell yeah."

"Shame you've been summoned like this." His dark eyes hinted at a desire to make me stay. "I was hoping for more fun this evening."

"It's fine. Annoying, but fine. This was great, thank you. And thanks for the shower. I honestly didn't expect anything at all."

Cade frowned. "Not expecting isn't the same as not deserving. It's the least I can do."

I nodded and shook myself into moving forward to kiss his cheek. "Thank you. That means a lot."

His arms came around me long enough for a quick hug before he steered me toward the counter and the door. "Go on then. My number's on the paper. Again, just in case."

Smiling, I picked up the folded paper and tucked it into my purse. "Thanks. For everything. I'll…see you around."

***

The situation at Callista's did anything but make me smile.

I walked into the bar in North Durham with my head high and my heels clacking, drawing a few raised eyebrows from the patrons in for some early drinks. A trio of elves in the corner narrowed their eyes at me before returning to their conversation.

The brick building almost reminded me of London, an English-style pub done in warm woods with a wraparound bar illuminated by dim lighting, backed by a mirror. Oversized Tarot cards hung on the wall, in what I suspected was a warning: the Wheel of Fortune, Justice, Death, the Tower, the Knight of Swords, the Seven of Wands, a few others. Maybe I was reading too much into something that might have been randomly chosen by the designer. But most of the cards spoke to either change, conflict, or people getting what was coming to them, and I really didn't see Callista trusting a space like this to anyone other than herself.

Sobered by the message in the cards, I made my way to the bar where the small, slim woman was filling drinks. I'd met Callista once, and it'd been more than enough for me never to want to do it again. Brown hair fell in waves to frame an averagely attractive face, but the cool green eyes were all she needed to get your attention.

Those eyes fell on me, flicking over me from head to toe as her eyebrows raised.

I clutched my purse and hesitated then pushed forward the rest of the way to the bar, not bothering to sit. "Callista."

"Good of you to make an appearance today, Lydia."

I winced. "It was my day off. I had plans."

She pursed her lips at that and eyed me again. "I see."

The petty bitch let me stew as she served a few more patrons then nodded me to the door at the back. I followed her through to another door. She breezed into a small office, with a heavy desk, an old desktop computer, and a Goddess-damned sword hanging from the back wall. I doubted she could wield it, given its size and hers, but it made a statement all the same.

"Sit." She dropped the reasonably pleasant demeanor she'd maintained at the bar.

"I'm good." I wasn't trying to antagonize her further, but she gave me the creeps and I was not about to get any closer to her than I had to.

Ire sparked in her gaze. Then she smiled, suddenly all sweetness. "Suit yourself. How are you finding your stay in the Triangle?"

I blinked at the shift, somehow feeling even more in danger than I had before. It took me a few seconds to find a reply. "It, ah—I'm good, thank you. What can I do for you, Callista?"

"Oh, so you *do* know you're here on my sufferance. Good. That'll make this easier."

Chills snuck over me. "Make what easier?"

"I might have a job for you. This is your interview." The look she gave my outfit was pure mean girl. "I suppose it's fitting you dressed up for it."

I ignored the barb. "What kind of job?"

"One suited for your particular skills."

"Oh?" My stomach did a flip, and my mouth dried. If Callista wanted to go around Farand and offer me bounty work directly, it'd put me in the shit with my direct boss but might achieve everything I'd been trying to do the long way with vampire connections.

"It's not confirmed yet. The client is evaluating their options, and I'm evaluating my resources. Talk to me about your Otherside hunts."

Business. We could talk business. I might be okay. "I've brought in high-blood elves, weres—mostly wolves—and a couple of vamps in their first or second centuries. A rogue selkie once." I hesitated then addressed the big issue. "I know I'm only a half-elf, but I'm good at my job. I can move more freely both among us and mundanes than most Othersiders, and I'm not afraid of big hunts."

From the flicker of her brows, she might have been impressed. "I see you understand my particular needs in this situation."

"Who's the target?" I wondered where she was going with this. Callista had said "the client," which could be anyone from any faction in the Triangle, especially if she was calling me in.

"It doesn't matter. The payoff will be worth your while."

"Excuse me?" I took a breath and swallowed my frustration, continuing again in a more respectful tone. "How am I supposed to know how to prep, or if this is even in my skill set, without knowing basic info about the target?" I was not prepared to take on a blank check bounty like this without knowing the details, even if I suspected I didn't really have a choice.

Then Callista said the magic words. "Because if you do this for me, I'll clear your exile debt with the Lyon Conclave of Queens and the local Houses."

I stiffened. Stared at her, my skin suddenly too tight and my heart beating too fast.

My freedom? Just like that?

I mean, I'd hoped for it to be an opportunity, but this was just being handed to me on a bloody silver platter.

There had to be a catch. There always was, something more than an obscure assignment. But she was dangling the one thing I wanted more than anything.

Still, I couldn't afford to be *too* reckless. "Why me?"

She tilted her head, her gaze as sharp as the sword on the wall behind her. "As you've noted, you have access to the entire territory, thanks to your particular situation, and you're better trained with more experience than the local talent with similar backgrounds. It provides an interesting opportunity."

"You don't have a Watcher to task with it?"

"The answer is in their name, my dear." Her expression hardened. "Any more questions? Because I won't offer this twice. You decide here and now."

I looked at the floor, as though I'd find the smart choice scratched in the wood floor, then met her gaze solidly.

Yeah, this was too good to be true.

But I was desperate enough to do it anyway. I had to get control of my life back. If the Arbiter would pay off the Lyon queens and House Monteague, my exile was effectively over. Better still, if I delivered, I'd also secure myself a patroness in Callista.

"I'll do the job," I said.

Her lips curled in a smile. "Sure about that? One way or another, it's your life on the line."

"Then it's not any different from any other day. I'm a half-elf in exile, Callista. You know what that means." All of my plans had my life on the line. My job, my half-baked ideas to work with the vampires for favors, offering blood in exchange for protection, fucking a vagabond, all of it. I'd take a chance at immediate freedom rather than spending the next who-knew-how-many years working for Farand or owing a debt to the vamps instead.

"Glad we can do business, child. Keep your phone handy, hm? If I have to wait four hours again, you'll regret it."

I nodded and fled with as much dignity as I could muster, equal parts relieved and shit scared.

Chapter 9: Cade

Cade started the evening resolved not to check his phone for a message from Lya. He also didn't go back to Nightshade, for fear that the third time *wouldn't* be the charm. Something had been wrong when she'd left his nest. She'd been unsettled, almost scared. More than he'd expect of a modern woman talking about her boss. It put him in mind of his youth on the high seas, answering to a ship captain who'd seemed all right, up to the moment it'd gone all wrong.

He didn't like it. Not for himself and not for her. They might only have slept together two nights and never exchanged blood, but his first instinct had been right, if for more reasons than he'd originally thought. Lya was indeed special and not just because of her blood. The fact that it'd been his initial focus shamed him a little. He would happily have glamoured and used her like he did the humans streaming ignorantly past him on the street, but then he'd brought her home. Seen that hint of secret unhappiness that didn't match the rest of her demeanor, before she'd refocused him on more carnal concerns.

There was real steel in her. A personality that could survive centuries, if she had them. It was forbidden to turn Othersiders, with good reason—the results were often unpredictable in the worst way. Weres would die outright. Witches would become one of the most terrifying undead, vampiric sorcerers. Elves had a fifty-fifty chance of going completely mad immediately or becoming too powerful for their sires to control.

But he had never heard anything about half-elves. They had human blood. Would that tip the odds toward success?

Don't even think it, he told himself. *Even if you are that lonely, she has a full life ahead of her.*

The inner turmoil kept him distracted as he wandered aimlessly to Moore Square. In the shadows near the burger place, he glamoured and drank from a couple, quick sips that could be mistaken for whispered conversation, hidden from casual view by the wide trunk of a pecan tree. A risk, especially when he could have just gone to one of Maria's clubs or drawn on the stash of blood in his closet fridge, but there was something restless stirring his feet and driving his thirst. Cade let the couple go on their way, acting casual as he leaned against the tree that had offered him cover.

A scent he hadn't smelled in ages teased his memory. Another *moroi*. One he'd thought long dead: his sire.

Can't be.

The wind shifted, and when it settled, the scent was gone like it'd never been. He frowned, wondering why he'd recall that particular scent when Lya had been on his mind all day. Fear, probably. His old captain had been the one to kill him, in the end. The one to bring him back. And the one to make him feel completely and utterly powerless, broken and beholden, locked in torture for his first two hundred years.

No.

Morris was gone. Cade had made sure of it.

Imagining the old bastard's smell now, sea salt and old blood blended with tobacco and semen and the iron-and-ash scent all vampires carried...it was the same thing that happened every time Cade found himself getting too comfortable. Feeling too safe. An instinctive reminder that he was, and could be, neither of those things. That he couldn't allow anyone close.

Which, he suspected, was a big part of why he felt such a connection to Lya. Whatever she was running from echoed a piece of his own past. One he'd been determined to gain enough power to leave behind but might be willing to face again if it meant spending part of his seemingly endless existence with someone like her.

Scrubbing a hand through his hair, Cade turned his feet toward Claret for the check-in he owed Aron. Maybe one of Torsten's *moroi* would do something shitty that'd give Cade the kick in the ass he needed to get the fuck out of Raleigh and quit this nonsense with Lya.

He could go to the coast. See the ocean again. Visit an old friend. Something to think about once he'd spoken to Aron.

Claret was packed when he got there, even on a Sunday night. Torsten's power signature pulsed faintly in the area, a metaphysical boundary marker any Othersider would sense. Cade bypassed the queue outside, flashing the business card that served as a membership ID with a nod to the *moroi* bouncer out front. No fucking around with human bouncers here, not at the entry to the coterie's nest. A few of the mundanes waiting to get in made disgusted comments, but he ignored them as he slipped into the slightly less humid atmosphere of the wine bar.

Maria was hard to spot among the taller patrons, but he caught a glimpse of her outrageous cobalt blue dye job on the other side of the room.

"Well, look who it is," she said when he made his way over to her. Her dark brown eyes held a hint of challenge. "Come to pay your respects in person?"

"I told you I'd be in. I know my obligations." Cade kept his voice low and tried not to loom.

Maria was tiny, not that she gave that impression. He was more conscious of the fact that she was as skilled as he with blades and more vicious with them, given that she was too small to cow anyone with her size. He was just enough older than her that he was confident he could take her, but he'd lose too much in the process.

"Do you?" she asked.

"Is this about Lya?"

Maria's attention sharpened. "Have you—"

"No, I haven't touched her blood."

She smiled. "Then no. Who are you here to see?"

"Aron. Or whoever needs an answer about the extension on my guest privileges."

"See, this is why I like you, Cade. You don't push your luck. Or your welcome."

He just stared at the smaller vampire. She was baiting him. He was sure of it. Doubly so when she grinned almost wide enough to flash fangs.

"Come on, grouchy-face. Goddess but you're dull these days. Must be something between the sheets to keep our Lya coming back to town two nights in a row though. I almost wish I was straight enough to want to find out."

"I won't insult you by pushing."

"I knew you were cleverer than you looked, pretty boy." She scoffed when he just stared at her again, even more flatly than before. "Fine. Come along."

She led him through the curtain concealing the short hallway to the lower levels of the bar then through the door at the end and down the spiral staircase. "Aron! Business call for you."

An average-height but beefy vampire with the same Viking styling as Torsten, only with a shorter, more modern hairstyle, slipped out of a room to the left after a short wait. "Must you shout so, Maria? A knock would do."

"But how would you know it was me?" She simpered at him, the look ringing fake to Cade. Likely to Aron too, given the vampire's long-suffering look.

"I'm sure the banging would do it," Aron said. "Back upstairs with you."

Maria hesitated, as though she wanted to argue to be brought in on their conversation, then made her way back up the stairs as regally as a queen. Aron watched her go, his expression blank enough that even Cade knew something was wrong.

Then Torsten's second waved Cade toward the door he'd just emerged from. "After you."

With a short, old-fashioned bow, Cade entered Aron's chambers. They weren't quite as stark as Torsten's, but they also lacked the roaring fireplace that made the cool dampness of being underground more tolerable. An intentional slight on Torsten's part, if Cade knew anything about the old bastard. After waiting for Aron's invitation, Cade settled on the edge of one of the room's plainly upholstered armchairs.

"I fear for what might happen to the coterie, should she succeed me," Aron said, seemingly absentmindedly as he sat in the chair adjacent to Cade's. The piercing look he leveled showed the lie though. "Are you sure you can't be convinced to join us?"

Cade barely controlled his frown. What the hell was going on with Aron that he was so sure Maria was on the verge of succeeding him? Apparently Oscar's comments in the club the other night hadn't been mere unquestioning support.

"It's a tempting offer," he said, only lying for the most part. Even without Lya in the picture, Cade wouldn't choose coterie life. Too many knew who and what he'd been after gaining his freedom from Morris for him to be safe. "But I'm afraid I must decline." He waited a polite moment before raising the issue he'd come here for. "As agreed, I've come to enquire about extending my guest rights. Do I have your permission to stay in the territory another six months?"

Aron heaved a breath he surely didn't need and clenched his hands, elbows on his knees as he leaned forward. "Unusual for vagabonds to stay as long as you have. What's it been? Two years now?"

"Eighteen months."

"So it will be two years."

Cade didn't answer. Both of them were capable of doing math.

"You're certain you don't simply want to join the coterie?"

"Quite. Thank you."

With a narrow-eyed sideways look, Aron asked, "Is this request for an extension anything to do with the half-elf Maria is currently so taken with?"

Cade held himself very still. "I hadn't realized she was that invested."

"So it is about the half-elf?"

"If it was?"

Aron snorted and shook his head. "Then I'd grant your request simply to be a pain in Maria's ass. She has ambitions I need to distract her from, given a few recent developments."

Easy choice politically, even if it made Cade feel more than a little gross. "I find Lya quite stimulating. I think she finds me similarly engaging, given that she came back for more the very next night."

The other vampire's relieved laugh at Cade's exaggerated, leering smile was exactly what he needed.

"Perfect. Fine. Extension granted. Fuck it, as long as you keep Maria occupied with retaining blood rights to that Goddess-burned half-elf, stay as long as you like."

Occupied, rather than eyeing your position as Torsten's second. Cade restrained himself from curling his lip in loathing, but the feeling snaked through his gut as much for Aron's weakness as his willingness to use Lya as a tool.

Politics disgusted him. Aron's apparent refusal simply to fight Maria made it worse. Using Lya's life and pleasure as a bargaining chip was the worst of all, especially when Cade reflected again on her brief moment of vulnerability the night before and what he knew of how the elves treated their low-blooded children.

She deserves better. Much better. She didn't ask for any of this.

With a broad, false smile that he pushed to look real, Cade forced himself to blank out the way elves spat on the half-elven and how vampires—including himself, he realized—fetishized them for their powerful elven blood and accessible human heritage.

He extended his hand to Aron.

And swore to himself he'd do better by Lya as Aron shook it.

It was another hour before Cade could make his excuses to leave without being rude. Maria gave him a weighing look that shifted to grudging respect when Cade inclined his head.

After a brief hesitation, he slid through the crowd to her, risking the deal he'd just made to salve his honor. "I told him what he needed to hear," he murmured to her. "Nothing more."

Maria's face flickered from disbelief to cunning before settling on a perfect blankness. "Always a pleasure, Cade."

He inclined his head again then made his way out.

Turmoil pushed him to wander Raleigh some more before heading home. He couldn't shake the anxiety the earlier scent had caused him, yet blood didn't interest him. He went back to Moore Square and walked the blocks around it, unable to let go of the idea that his sire might not actually be dead.

At the corner of Hargett and Person, a man dressed in torn clothing, smelling of marijuana, stirred from where he lay on a bench. "Hey. Hey man."

Cade shook his head. "Sorry, I don't—"

"You're Cade."

He froze. "Where did you hear that name, and why do you think it's me?"

"Yeah, yeah I thought so. Look just like he said. I have a message for you."

Torn between wanting to deny it and paranoia driving him to get answers, Cade chose answers. "Like who said? What message?"

"Ol' white dude said, 'You'll have to do better next time if you want to be rid of me, boy. I'll see you again soon.'" The man badly mimicked a London accent.

The cold chill of the grave iced through Cade. Only one person had ever called him 'boy' in his life, and Cade had only ever tried to be rid of that same person. Morris. *Impossible.*

The man was looking at him expectantly.

"Is that all?" Cade said between gritted teeth.

"Yep. That's all." He scowled. "What, you ain't even got a tip for me?"

Glamouring him would be safer, but he looked like one of those the city had left behind. Lips pressed tight, Cade pulled out his wallet and handed over a twenty.

"All right, all right, thanks, man!" The bill disappeared into the pocket of his torn jeans before the man laid back down on the bench. "You have a good night now."

"And you." Cade hurried away, pulling a strong glamour to turn attention away from him as he did.

There were a few people from his past who'd known Morris. Was this a sick joke? Vengeance for what he'd done after escaping? A setup for a bribe attempt? Was he being hunted?

86

Maybe it was time to move on. The more he thought about leaving, though, the more pissed off he got. He was finally finding something good, and he'd be damned if some prankster thought a vampire with five centuries could be chased off like some new-made fledgling. The extension of his guest privileges should have pleased him, given that it meant more time to win Lya over, but all he felt was a simmering outrage that slipped into churning guilt as his thoughts shifted from himself to her.

Was he wrong for wanting Lya? Seeking powerful blood was in his nature, even if he'd found himself moving beyond that. It was part of how he survived in a world where vampires could only live so long before the virus started failing to repair cellular deterioration, with the brain being the first organ to go, given the amount of resources it consumed. Those who took the risk to hunt and feed on Othersiders lived millennia. Those who subsisted on human blood alone managed a few centuries at most, if they survived their fledgling decade.

Nothing was meant to live forever, no matter how much it tried.

But the chance to live a few more years—months, even— with a being he was already coming to respect for her toughness and sense of self? That couldn't be wrong. He hoped. Was wanting her for more than blood better or worse, if she was effectively a tool either way?

As he made his way up the stairs to his nest, his phone buzzed in his pocket. He stopped in mid-step at the text message attached to an unknown number.

I keep thinking of your arms around me, it said, *and other parts in me.*

A second message dinged after the first.

This is Lya btw. In case you're that kind of player.

Well. If she was just as interested, it definitely couldn't be wrong.

Could it?

He jogged up the stairs, blowing into his apartment and shutting the door behind him, locking it firmly. The blackout curtains were still shut from earlier, and Cade skipped the shower to throw himself into the bed that still smelled of her as he composed a reply.

Deleted it. Tried again. Deleted and redrafted.

Some of the older *moroi* were hopeless with technology newer than a century after their death, but he'd made a point of keeping up with innovation and change. Vagabonds didn't have the luxury of being Luddites.

What makes you think I'm seeing other people? Other than for the obvious.

He hesitated, debating whether to send it. *Moroi* always kept their options open. Always. In blood and in bed, even within a coterie, unless a special someone was chosen as a solidaire. Suggesting he was doing anything to the contrary would be exposing himself in a way that felt dangerous…except she'd already shown a piece of herself in this same bed.

Cade stabbed his thumb down on the send button before he could change his mind.

If nothing else, it would take his mind off the creeping sense of danger from the night's mysterious messenger.

Chapter 10: Lya

Why the hell am I tempting a vampire? Stupid. Stupid.

Except that Shonda had sent a message asking what'd happened after I'd insisted on leaving the club alone, and even the extremely edited recounting I'd given her had sent warmth spreading through my lower parts.

Fuck it. I liked Cade. He treated me like a person. Like what I wanted—and more importantly, what I needed—mattered.

Yeah, it was a low bar, but still.

I considered the last two nights as I lounged on my sofa, debating whether to hit the gym or give myself a night to recover.

Vampires were apex predators. The older ones in particular had spent centuries killing to survive and had come from times when lives were less valuable and more violently disposable to those who had power. Was Cade just a good actor? I couldn't tell. That part worried me. But the part of me that was dangerously lonely and hungry for what he was showering on me didn't care.

You're opening yourself up for another hard lesson, Lya.

I shook off the inner voice, the pessimist in me that was still holding on to past hurts. What if we could work something out? Would I take the risk?

My phone dinged.

What makes you think I'm seeing other people? Other than for the obvious.

I stared at the text.

Did that say what I thought it was saying? That other than taking what blood he needed, he wasn't actively seeing anyone else? Did he mean consistently or at all?

I swung myself to sit upright then got up to pace when I was too full of energy to sit.

Are you flirting with me? I sent back after a few minutes.

Cade replied immediately. *Is it welcomed?*

I flushed. Hesitated. Went for honesty. *Hell yes.*

In that case, I would very much like to continue having parts of me around you. And in you. Preferably soon.

If I thought I was flushing before, I was on fire now. I stared at my phone with my eyes popping out of my head. A vampire. Sexting. It inspired me to be forward; I didn't believe in playing hard to get. There was always another man if this one turned out to be an asshole.

Then take me on a date. A real one. My heart thundered as I waited for his response.

What do you like? Outside of bed, that is, although I would like to hear more about any special requests in that arena as well.

I grinned, feeling wicked. *Surprise me.*

Very well. Tuesday at 8pm?

Just tell me where.

I'll arrange a car. Smart casual. See you Tuesday, beautiful.

I sent him a confirmation and, after hesitating long enough to debate it, my address. Then I danced around my living room, inexplicably happy and excited rather than paranoid and scared.

An actual date. My first one since moving here.

I decided to skip the gym and turned on some music before pouring a glass of wine. Yeah, it was more than a little risky to keep playing this game with him. I didn't care. I wanted to live my life, even if it was short and disgraced. I wanted to feel good, even if it was dangerous. I'd steal joy for myself, even if it was at the point of a vampire's fangs.

Joy felt like rebellion, and I wanted more of it.

***

The next morning, joy felt more like a hangover. I still didn't care. I drove to the office with a pounding head and a lightness in my heart I couldn't remember feeling for ages. Even sitting in the car for an extra minute to tamp it down before Farand could see it and steal it from me didn't kill my mood.

On impulse, I sent Cade a quick message before I got out of the car. *I like when you hold me down and have your way.*

Tucking my phone away, I headed into the office, barely remembering to smother my grin again as I walked in the door.

Farand was, predictably, in a shitty mood even for a Monday and seemed inclined to take it out on me. "You're late."

I glanced at the clock on the wall and bit my lip to stop myself from pointing out that three minutes past nine was hardly late.

"Traffic," I muttered instead.

He glared, tapping his foot as the others bent their heads and looked busy. "What did Callista want?"

The other half dozen people in the office went quiet.

I swallowed, taken aback by the question. Nobody spoke about what happened between them and Callista when summoned. Even the summoning was meant to stay limited to whoever had carried it out.

"That's not your business." I should have handled it better, but I was slightly hungover, more than a little furious, and still riding the high of the weekend's events.

If I'd thought everyone was quiet before, they were utterly silent now.

"Excuse me?" Farand said.

Gritting my teeth, I assumed the parade rest anyone trained by the elves fell into on reflex when confronted and trying to look less threatening. The words that came out of my mouth were combative enough. "If she wanted everyone to know, she'd have summoned everyone. Sir."

The look on Farand's face should have struck the fear of the Goddess into me, but all I could think was that he looked scared himself. Scared of becoming irrelevant. That I, the half-elf, might have made myself more valuable to the Arbiter somehow.

"If that's how you want to play it," Farand said after a tense pause.

"Farand—"

"No, I see how this is going. Play the big leagues then, halfling. See where it gets you."

The slur took me aback. "What did you—"

"You heard me. Now sit the fuck down and get to work, or I'll need to have a word with the Conclave of Lyon about how well you're holding up the terms of your exile."

I stood there, jaw clenched so tightly I thought my teeth would shatter as my blood flushed hot from head to toe. I fisted my hands behind my back, hard enough for my nails to dig into my palms.

Farand just watched with an ugly sneer, even as he tensed and the lines of his stance shifted ever so slightly, reminding me of something I'd forgotten. He was Darkwatch-trained—badly out of favor at court, but there was a reason he'd been shifted to bounty hunting and not something less dangerous.

He was goading me on purpose, hoping to push me into reacting violently in a room full of witnesses. At which point he could use both his training and his stronger Aether to beat the hell outta me and pull one of the mind-tricks the Monteagues and my mother's House Desmarais were renowned for, likely making me humiliate myself further. I knew from experience how bad that would be, and I also knew that, while I was strong for a half-elf, I couldn't beat a full-blooded elf magically in a fair fight.

For a minute, I was tempted to try him anyway, but I wasn't ready. Soon but not yet. And I wouldn't let this bastard think he could push my buttons, no matter how much it infuriated me even further to play the elven game of Houses.

I did let a nasty smile of my own curl my lips, fueled by what Cade had said last night: *"Whatever you need, I can give you."*

Even if Callista was playing me for a fool, I had my out. I just had to bide my time and stop worrying about my feelings long enough to wrap the vampire around my little finger. I could do that. I could do anything.

Including swallow my pride and let Farand win this particular battle.

"Of course," I said as coolly as he'd been when he'd spat venom at me. "Excuse me."

He nearly snarled as I backed up a step and signaled that I wasn't going to take his poisoned bait.

I turned my back on him and made my way to my desk, my sneakers almost soundless on the tile floor and my head high as I ignored the other bond-running bounty hunters and took my seat. None of them had said a word in support, just watched like gormless cowards.

They were beneath me. All of this was beneath me.

I was playing a game that had been stacked against me from the beginning, thinking all I had to do to win was follow the rules and bide my time. But there was another option: blow it the fuck up.

No more playing other people's games. From now on, I play my own.

I looked at Farand one last time when I felt eyes on me from his desk. Pure antagonism radiated from him as he glared at me.

I didn't understand it in the least. I'd done nothing to him. I hadn't even been anything to him until I was assigned here.

Was that it? Did he feel slighted by having to babysit an exiled half-elf?

Tough shit for him. That was a him problem that he was making a me problem. I let amusement seep into my return stare before putting my eyes back on my computer screen and settling in to do some research.

Slowly, the office returned to its usual low murmur of conversation and ringing phones.

The day crawled by. I ignored my phone, grabbed lunch from the empanada place around the corner, ate at my desk, and stayed exactly twenty-three minutes past six—my lunch plus the time I was supposedly late.

It was just me and Farand when I rose to go, the rest of our colleagues having caught the tone of the day and wanting to be elsewhere.

"You really think you're as good as us, don't you?" Farand hissed as I approached the door.

"No," I said defiantly as I pushed it open. "I'm better."

I kept going before he could reply. That was going to cost me, even if it was true. I had to be better. I had to be smarter and tougher and bolder.

Surviving with half the magic in Otherside had always been a chancy life. The fact that it'd become more so today settled me into a strange calm. This was what I lived for. The fight. Now I finally had my avenue for it.

I took a different route home than usual, just in case Farand had some of his old Darkwatch buddies on standby to cause an "accident" that would, at the very least, get me dinged on my car insurance. I was almost surprised when there was nobody waiting in the parking lot or at my apartment. A glance at my

Secrets and Truths

phone showed a few missed texts, including one with an image from Cade, and I forced myself not to look at it. Gym first.

I got my strength training in, pushing hard. Between fucking a vampire and my boss attempting to fuck me over, I figured I'd be glad of it sooner or later. Only when I was sucking down a peanut butter cup smoothie on my way out did I allow myself to read my messages.

Cade's earned me an annoyed beep when I stopped in the middle of the parking lot.

The man was both an artist and a work of art, somehow managing to send a nude selfie that was both tasteful and erotic. Definitely better than a crude dick pic.

I waved an apology at the motorist and hustled to jog home. It was less than half a mile. I could manage it in five minutes even with a belly full of smoothie. I made it faster than usual, despite the red light at the crossing on 54, spurred by a desire to review that photo more closely.

When I'd slammed and locked the door behind me—and shoved a chair under the knob just to make myself feel better— I sent a reply.

Well, damn. That's exactly what I needed after a day like today. Better than the gym session I just had for getting my mind right.

The reply came back as I was stripping for my shower. *Here I was worried that I'd overstepped. What happened?*

I hesitated. I was genuinely not in the mood for sympathy, even if it was coming from a good place—but one that didn't understand my experience. At the same time, I wanted to tell him. I wanted to be comforted and told that Farand was as much of an asshole as I thought he was. I could fight my own battles, but I was starting to like the idea of having someone to hold my hand and watch with me while the world burned.

95

I bit my lip and settled on a summarized version. *My boss crossed several lines knowing my hands are tied. The kind of lines that mean blood.*

The gif that came back chased my bad mood away to make me cackle: a brunette woman outside a window, pointing at a handwritten cardboard sign that read, "Want me to kill them?"

A sexting vampire who also had a grasp on meme culture. How the fuck old was he? And where had he picked all this up? Vampires usually struggled with staying modern.

I'm tempted. Then, in a burst of daring—*Keep making me laugh like this, and I'll send nudes.*

This time the gif was that animated Puss from one of the Shrek movies, which made me laugh all the harder for the fact that it was the precursor to the damn cat pulling out a sword and thrashing some assholes.

You win. Stay tuned.

I wait with bated breath and a rather hard cock.

I grinned. *Prove it.*

Chapter 11: Lya

I survived the next working day, arriving early and leaving bang on time. Fortunately, a few mundane runs took me out of the office, keeping Farand and me out of each other's space for most of the day. I took my time on the paperwork at the jail as well.

Because fuck him.

I sped home, again taking a different route and glad that I wouldn't be driving my own car tonight. Farand couldn't really do anything to me while Callista had an interest, but Callista hadn't told me what she wanted yet and played favorites like roulette. The safety of limbo was minimal, and either way, I'd pass out of favor as soon as I quit being useful. I needed a plan together before then.

Cade had said business casual. As I searched my closet for something dressy but not too dressy, I asked myself again what I wanted from this. Was he just a means to an end? A dependable fuckbuddy? Or did I want something more…real? Something more than to use and discard?

I might plow into shit headlong, but I did my best to figure out what I wanted from it. That was the only way to know when it was time to go. But it'd been so long since I'd had to ask myself that I suspected I was thinking with my sex drive. Because the only answer I could honestly give myself was driven by the picture of him lounging in an overstuffed armchair, cock in hand, as those dark eyes promised whatever I had the courage to ask for.

Fuck it. I wouldn't be dressed for long if I had my way. I grabbed my newest pair of black jeans and a dark red sleeveless blouse. The low, narrow vee in front was echoed by a wider but even lower vee in the back. I wouldn't be able to wear a bra, but that'd never stopped me before. Once dressed, I wrangled my curls into place with a little product and threw my silver knives in my purse, just in case.

Finally, I heard an expensive engine pull up out front. A peek out the window showed a sleek, black car idling as the driver stepped out. Slipping on my nice black heels, I grabbed my purse and headed out.

"Lya?" the driver called.

"That's me."

He got the door, and I slid into the embrace of nice leather seats, paying half a mind as he told me to help myself to water or the little squares of Ghirardelli chocolates. After a quick thank you, I texted Cade to let him know I was on my way.

Good. Hope you like Mexican food.

I grinned, equal parts flattered and amused. He was really gonna try to do a date-date for my benefit? Something relatively normal?

Cade waited in front of the two-story restaurant we pulled up to in RTP, one of the fancier Mexican places. He was dressed similarly to me, in nice-looking, dark-wash jeans and a midnight blue shirt with a silvery shimmer to it, sleeves half-rolled and top three buttons undone. It was a far more casual look than the suits he'd worn to the club. More accessible in a way that was somehow even hotter.

I thanked the driver and slid out as Cade approached to murmur a few words and hand over a tip.

"Don't you look good enough to eat," he said teasingly when he rejoined me.

"You're making it hard to think about much else, to be honest."

"Good." He leaned close to whisper, sending a warm breath over my neck to make me shiver as he steered me toward the doors with a hand at the small of my back. "I'd never push you into anything you don't want to do, but I'm not above a little temptation."

I snorted. "A little?"

Cade just smiled and got the door. After a minute, we were led out to the patio, to a table in the corner under a red canvas umbrella. Privacy from above and the plants lining the fence offered more from the street.

"Okay?" Cade asked. When I nodded, he got my chair for me.

"Always a gentleman."

"Or the product of an older time." He flashed a smile and took his seat, eyes roving as he adjusted his chair so that it was both closer to mine and afforded him a better view of anyone approaching.

I decided to test him. "How much older?"

He studied me, almost suspiciously, before an amused smile curled his lips. "Let's just say my earliest memories of this side of the ocean are of fighting over Puerto Rico."

I wasn't familiar with the history of the Americas so I filed that away for later, wondering why he was acting more on edge than usual. Performance anxiety? Worried about being away from Raleigh? RTP was neutral territory, but it did edge pretty close to some elven and werecat zones. As powerful as he was, he was probably just wary about running into more Othersiders and starting an inter-factional flare-up.

The arrival of the server distracted me from asking. I skimmed the menu quickly and ordered steak tacos and a margarita then looked expectantly at Cade. What the hell did vampires do on a date?

"Just a water with lemon and appetizers for me, thanks." He looked more amused than ever. "Guacamole will be great."

After the server left, I looked at him with lifted brows. "You actually gonna—"

"Of course. Avocados are high in antioxidants. Not as nutritious as my usual fare and not something I could survive on, but we would have died out if we couldn't blend in reasonably well."

"Well shit. Learn something new every day."

Dinner passed quickly, with Cade utterly charming me with stories of his youth. He'd apparently spent a lot of time at sea trying not to fall overboard or in ports foreign to him, playing the bumbling fool. I didn't buy any of it, not fully, but I enjoyed the storytelling nonetheless. Before I knew it, we were done eating. He paid the bill without letting me see it, and I let him. He had the power and the wealth in this situation, after all.

"What would you like to do now?" he asked as we stood out front. "I have some ideas if you want more surprises."

I went up on tiptoes and kissed him. "In the mood for a little after-dinner entertainment?"

Something hungry entered his gaze. "What did you have in mind?"

"Dancing. The horizontal kind."

"Your place or mine?"

"Yours." I was familiar with it now, and I'd rather do the trip back to Durham from Raleigh than let him into my space just yet.

Something I couldn't read flickered behind his eyes, but all he said was, "My place it is."

The same driver who'd brought me to the restaurant drove us to Raleigh while we bantered and flirted in the back seat. I was on Cade as soon as he'd shut and locked the door to his place behind us. His hands skimmed up under my shirt just as quickly, and he made a low growl of pleasure at finding me bare under it.

"I wondered what kind of sartorial magic was going on with a back like that. Clearly I was overthinking."

I didn't bother to reply, busying myself with getting the buttons of his shirt and jeans open so that I could kiss and nibble on his skin. He lifted me easily, and I wrapped my legs around his waist, still kissing him as he carried me to the bedroom.

The mutual urgency to our stripping reassured me that, even if I was aroused beyond reason by all this, he was too. I'd barely gotten my clothes off before he was on me, pinning me to the bed as he suckled on a nipple. The slightest graze of sharp teeth made me gasp, but I trusted him not to bite. The fact that he might tripped the twisted part of my brain that found that arousing though, and I arced my hips up against him.

My phone chose that moment to go off with a text notification. I ignored it. Then another came through.

Cade eased away. "Should you check that?"

"I'm busy."

"Given what happened last time you missed a message here…"

He was right, and Callista had said to keep my phone handy. With a groan for the interruption, I rolled and hung over the edge of the bed, patting the floor for my jeans and the phone in the butt pocket. I found and unlocked it, frowning at the blocked number and the message. A bounty.

With the face of the man I'd just fallen into bed with attached.

Wanted, preferred alive. Cade, M, age approximately 500 years. Faction: Vampire. Status: Unaffiliated - vagabond. Note: Assume armed *and very dangerous. Bounty: $500,000 alive, $250,000 destroyed (evidence required).*

This had to be the one Callista had told me to wait for. The stakes were never that high, even for a were on the full moon or an elf at the new moon. Someone wanted Cade bad, enough to pay a premium, even on a vampire hunt. My heart sank and adrenaline shot through me, sending my heart racing faster than Cade's touch had.

I did my best to keep my breathing even, not wanting to tip him off. What the fuck had I gotten myself in the middle of?

"Something wrong?"

"No." I cleared the notice, locked my phone, dropped it on my jeans, and rolled back up to give him my prettiest smile.

His dark eyes flicked over me as he inhaled. Then he smiled back, the edge to it hard enough to make me shiver. "Good. I wanted to make you an offer."

"Oh yeah? What's that?"

Cade didn't look away from me as he eased closer, as smooth as a snake with whatever blood he'd taken before coming to meet me. Goosebumps rippled over me as he traced a finger over my belly and up between my breasts—then closed his hand around my throat and squeezed on either side of my windpipe. I could breathe, but I'd pass out if I didn't move fast.

"You tell me why you got shit scared just now. I don't drain you."

I reacted on instinct, rolling my lower body up explosively to aim a kick at his head. His dodge loosened his grip from my throat enough that I was able to tear free. I scrambled to get off the bed and to the knife in my purse, sitting at the front door.

His grip closed around my ankle and hauled me back just as my fingers brushed the hardwood floor. This time, he trapped me under his body, stretching full length over me, and pinned my wrists over my head with one big hand. The other gripped my jaw and wrenched my head to the side, exposing a long stretch of my neck.

"That was rude, Lya," he said. "It is really Lya, right?"

I gave him my third-best smile—as good as I could, given his fingers pressing into my cheeks—and tried to calm my pounding heart before the thumping vein in my throat gave him more ideas. "Actually, yeah. For once."

"Good. Seems to me that it wasn't just my charming personality that brought you to my bed, so why don't we start over. What the fuck is a half-elf with combat training doing scouting in Raleigh, and what message did you get just now that made you ready to fight?"

My mind raced. He thought I'd been coming back to Raleigh to scout? Was this why he'd been weird at dinner? Not because of territory risks but because he knew he was being hunted?

Shit.

If he knew someone was after him, it was my bad luck that he'd already been tipped off, and I didn't have many options. Cade was bigger than me, stronger, faster, and had me properly pinned down.

I hadn't come out hunting. I'd come out for a date. That meant I was low on options—meaning weapons. Shit did not look good, and I'd made it worse.

"Well?" Cade's breath was warm against my ear. "I'm waiting, beautiful."

Truth or dare? Sometimes they were one and the same. "It was a message from Callista." Let him infer my purpose in Raleigh from that.

"Hekate burn it," he cursed in a low growl. "What did you come here for?"

Truth was easy this time, and it hurt, both because I should have known better than to let my libido dictate my decisions and because I did genuinely like him. "To fuck you, you asshole! We were on a *date*!"

"Then what scared you?"

Now for the lie that would let me walk out of here until I could figure out what the fuck to do. "Goddess save me, have you met Callista? She's summoned me. Tomorrow. I've only met her the once, and she scared the shit out of me."

Sharp teeth pricked the pulse points on the right side of my throat. "Are you lying?"

I shivered at the movement of his lips against my skin, as intimate as they'd been before but in a different way. "Am I in a position to lie right now? Goddess, Cade. In case the accent didn't tip you off, I'm not from around here. Sometimes it seems like I have obligations to half the Triangle. Including Callista."

The prick of his teeth withdrew as he pulled away to study me with narrowed eyes and scenting nostrils.

"Killing me will be more trouble than it's worth," I said, just in case he didn't reach the conclusion I needed him to. "You really want to risk stirring up the queens in Chapel Hill? Or pissing off Callista? You might have some protection from reprisal as a vagabond, but I think Torsten would take drastic measures to keep the peace. He'd turn you over or behead you himself, whichever the offended party preferred."

My heart thudded as Cade thought that over. I think we both knew the queens wouldn't give a shit about me, but Callista might, if she was interested enough to be summoning me.

"Luckily for you, I agree. And I..." Dark hair fell over his eyes as he tilted his head and continued to study me. Not freeing me yet, but not as active a threat as before. If anything, he looked part confused and part ashamed.

I didn't let myself relax though. Fast as I was, vampires—and all full-blood Othersiders—were faster. He could have his fangs in my neck as quickly as I could blink if he changed his mind.

Not only that but he could make me like it as he killed me.

He sighed, and his grip eased. "You have to know I've grown fond of you, Lya. Enough that I'd protect you."

"Don't," I whispered, frustrated as hell. This could have been something good, and it'd gone so wrong. "Don't do that. You have no idea what you're promising."

I had an idea though, of what it could mean to choose his protection. I shuddered, remembering nights in Maria's arms. The spiraling pleasure of glamour masking the blood loss. Trusting that Maria preferred a repeated harvest over time to getting a big boost all at once. Trust I wanted to extend to Cade but was afraid to because my feelings for him had started to run much deeper than just a casual fuck. Trust I couldn't extend because now I had to figure out how to bring him in.

Whatever he took that small movement for, he got all the way off me. As soon as I was free, I rolled off the bed and retreated to the bedroom door.

"Lya, I'm sorry," he said. "I had to be sure. There's been a recent development. Suffice to say, I have reason to seriously doubt my safety."

He was clearly right to, but it didn't lessen the outrage that always flickered in me when a man thought he could try that shit with me.

"You know what? Save it. Thanks for dinner. I'm going to call it a night."

"Lya—"

Ignoring the note of dismay in his tone, I darted closer to my clothes and snagged the heap, retreating again to yank them on. I needed to get home and regroup. When my head popped out of my shirt, he was on his knees in front of me. I jumped backward, not having heard him move.

"I would never take anything from you, not your secrets or truths, not your body or blood, without your permission."

"Oh please. You wouldn't have hesitated to take everything if you hadn't liked my answer."

"Which would be within my rights if you had been planning to harm me." Dark eyes begged my understanding and forgiveness, even as his face pinched with frustration. I got the feeling he wanted to believe what he was saying. Maybe even did, even if it was all somewhat contradictory.

He wasn't wrong, and I was now contracted to bring him in—which would almost certainly cause him harm. I hated everything about the situation I'd put myself in. And yet, guilt weighed heavy. It was just shitty luck that our situations were intersecting like this.

I couldn't do this. I couldn't stand here and hash out the fact that, yes, I was supposed to be hunting him, when I couldn't trust he'd handle himself without draining me. So, of course, I did the only thing I could do.

Nope, not be an adult and talk about it.

I got my shit together and left, slamming the door behind me and trying to blink away hot tears.

Chapter 12: Cade

Cade stayed kneeling after Lya left, staring at the floor without seeing it. Both blood and passion had gone cold in him, leaving only the gut-wrenching feeling that he'd fucked up. Badly. The day's sleep had been soaked in half-remembered nightmares of blood, pain, and humiliation, brought on by that hint of a scent that had reminded him of his sire and the bizarre message he'd received. When Lya'd had her quiet adrenaline spike over whatever was in that message, he'd jumped to a conclusion: that she was somehow part of some plot on his life.

It had made sense in the three seconds it had taken the idea to form in his mind. She'd never mentioned what she actually did for work. Half-elves knew better than to risk coming to Raleigh. They knew they were fair game. Most weren't bold enough to make the arrangement Lya had with Maria, or they weren't desperate enough.

Lya was. Which of the two he didn't know, but she was.

And then for her to come to his bed twice in as many nights? Ask for a date the night after he'd caught a scent that should've been long dead? Fear had screamed that maybe his sire wasn't really dead. That Cade had to be a target and Lya the huntress.

Or so he'd thought.

Of course, she could have been lying. It was exactly what a bounty hunter pretending not to be one would do.

But if that was the case, why hadn't she taken him already? Two nights in a row, he'd passed out in a sated sexual exhaustion the likes of which he hadn't experienced in at least a century, and she'd been right alongside him, little silver knives and all.

No, it didn't make sense for her to have missed two easy chances.

He'd caught a little of the voice Lya had been speaking to the other day and it hadn't been Callista, but a summons from that hag would be enough to give any Othersider a jolt. Lya was only half-Otherside, walking a precarious line on the best of days. She probably practiced martial arts to defend herself from the kind of shit he himself had pulled, a necessary precaution when everyone in the world she walked in was faster, stronger, or more magically gifted than she was.

"Fuck," he snarled. Then again, louder, because the word just didn't sum up the magnitude of what he was feeling.

It was only while watching her stalk out the door in a righteously cold fury that he realized he was definitely feeling more than bloodlust or sexual attraction for her. It might only have been a few days since they'd met, but he'd been alone long enough to know when he'd come across someone special.

Lya was a once-in-a-century kind of person, maybe rarer, and he'd let his paranoia and the bloody ghosts of his past scare her off.

Cade dragged himself to his feet, snatched a robe from behind the door, and slipped it on, not bothering to tie it shut. He had to make this right. But he had to do it without pushing himself on her or scaring her or…or even assuming that she'd want to see him again at all. He'd pushed her tonight, and she'd run.

He sighed and slumped against the kitchen counter, scrubbing his hands over his face.

First though, he needed to set his mind at ease. That meant figuring out if his sire was indeed still alive, once and for all. Not only that but in town, stalking Cade for revenge, or if this was someone else playing a twisted game or seeking their own vengeance.

Morris deserved everything I did to him.

It wasn't just his own mind saying that Cade had been fully justified in what he'd done. The Otherside maxim of an eye for an eye and blood for blood said that he had been within his rights to take justice in blood, to the point of death. The familiar thoughts didn't do anything to reassure him though. If Morris had survived being staked through the heart and set on fire, Cade was in trouble.

Worse, if he'd survived, tracked Cade to Raleigh, and been watching, this nest might be compromised. Which meant Lya would be in danger as well.

Icy fear, the kind Cade remembered viscerally but hadn't experienced in hundreds of years, clawed through his veins.

This is intolerable.

He hadn't survived this long to be done in by a dead tyrant or lose the one being that'd sparked a sense of life into him in centuries over paranoia. Cade strode back to the bedroom and dressed in fresh clothes: lighter-colored jeans, a T-shirt, and a hoodie. The muggy evening was slightly too warm for humans to wear hoodies, so he might draw notice, but combined with a red cap blazoned with the wolf mascot of the local university, it'd hide his features and make people assume he was just another college kid.

College kid. He'd been a little older than that when Morris had killed him for his pretty face and devil-may-care attitude, saying it was perfect for immortality. What Cade had really been perfect for was certain of Morris's abusive predilections.

No. Never again.

The past would stay in the past, even if Cade had to burn it twice, and the present would be just as dead if someone here and now thought they could fuck with him. He headed out, changing everything about the way he walked and the route he took back to Moore Square. If Morris was indeed still alive, he'd catch the iron-and-ash scent of a fellow *moroi*, but hopefully think that Cade was one of Torsten's.

Then again, if Cade could remember Morris's scent, he might not be that lucky. Still, he had to check, for his sanity and Lya's safety.

The square was busy again. It should be winding down, given that it officially closed at ten, but tell that to the people enjoying their evening. A few intoxicated mundanes brushed past, tempting him to top up the blood he'd taken before the ill-fated date, but he kept himself focused. Sorting out whatever his fucking problem was with the ghost of Morris had to be done before he did anything to pursue Lya further. He couldn't let his issues be hers.

As he walked, letting mind and senses drift, he tried to set aside fears and doubts. There was no scent where he'd been last night, so he kept moving, trying to move in a search grid without it being obvious that he was doing so. The more he cast about and found nothing, the more he told himself he was being unforgivably paranoid.

Until he caught the hint of a scent at the corner of Hargett and Person, the same place he'd come across the strange messenger last night.

Cade froze, disbelieving. The scent was definitely another *moroi*. Not one of Torsten's. Cade had been in the area long enough to learn the shared scent of the coterie. Warily, he followed it east down Hargett Street, skin crawling as it grew stronger the closer he got to the City Cemetery.

This can't be right. He can't be in Raleigh.

But the scent only grew heavier, as though Morris not only was in Raleigh but had been staying, rather stereotypically, in or near the cemetery. Cade's heart didn't need to beat, but it did now, gearing him up for fast action. He turned left, following his nose up South East Street and then cautiously through the gates of the cemetery.

A low, whisper-soft voice to his left pulled his attention. "This is the longest you've stayed in one place in over a century, boy."

Cade spun to find Morris leaning irreverently against a tombstone a few feet away.

His sire's tall, once-powerful frame was withered beyond recognition, as though the fire that hadn't killed him had simply consumed every ounce of flesh on him. A white linen suit hung from him, giving the vampire the appearance of a cheap wire clothes hanger. Bright blue eyes flashed in the beam of a passing headlight, peering from under the brim of a white Panama hat. Stringy, white hair that must have been in patches hung unevenly to Morris's shoulders, a far cry from the thick, black abundance it had once been. Glamour hovered around him in an invisible miasma, lapping at Cade's mind and seeking a way in, and a dog started barking as the woman walking it outside the fence abruptly recoiled at the sensation and went in the other direction.

It was like seeing a living ghost.

Cade gaped, unable to find words. He'd been certain Morris was dead. Two hundred years of torture had given him plenty of time to plan his strike, and when his moment had come, he'd stabbed his sire with silver then staked him, dumped him in a pit, poured pitch over him, and watched the old bastard burn until he'd stopped screaming...but had been forced to flee when he'd heard human voices.

He'd never taken the man's head.

"Nothing to say to your sire after all these years?" Morris stepped toward him.

That movement pulled a word from Cade's tongue. "Stop."

Looking amused, the other *moroi* did, leaning on another tombstone as though he'd collapse without one holding him up and casting a leering eye over Cade. "You look like you're keeping well. That's good. You owe me blood, boy. It's time to come home now."

"I won't. Never." Cade glanced around, trying to gauge how many humans were in range.

Too many. In the open like this, there was no way he could kill another vampire, dispose of the body, and not get caught by either the humans living in the nice new buildings across the street or the Watchers Callista was rumored to have in the area.

"Why aren't you dead?" Cade asked.

Morris ignored him. "I thought you might come looking after you got my message, and here you are. Something must have caught your interest for you to stay. Is it the woman? Maybe I should pay her a visit. Or better still, see what price Callista wants for her. Your little halfling bitch is a mighty fine specimen. Looks like she'd go down a treat after a bit of…fun. You remember what fun we used to have, don't you? Think your woman could survive it?" He leered again. "Or even enjoy it?"

Cade clenched his fists, mindful of the human habitations surrounding them and the rules of the Détente. If he did anything to expose Otherside, it'd cost him his life. Morris knew it. He was almost certainly counting on it.

The thin, burn-scarred skin of the old bastard's face pulled taut as he smiled, exactly as Cade remembered. It was a more terrifying look now though, all hollow cheeks and impotent rage.

"That's right," Morris said. "Mustn't let the ignorant cattle know of our existence, hm? But don't worry. I owe you a thrashing that'll make you wish you'd taken my head and killed me properly. If you survive it, that is. Now if you'll excuse me, dear boy, I have some preparations to make. See you soon. Maybe her too, hm?"

Glamour flared, and Cade flinched, trying to back out of range. But it was useless. The telepathic link between sire and fledgling was too strong at this distance. Morris weighed him down with the mental pressure any sire could impose to addle their fledgling and seemingly disappeared.

"Fuck," Cade snarled when his mind cleared.

He didn't bother trying to figure out where Morris had gone. The master vampire could be far away, or he might be close by still, hoping to draw Cade into an ambush. He probably had somewhere else to stay the night as well, just in case Cade did manage to track him here.

Worse, he couldn't go to Maria with this. Not yet. If the coterie knew Morris was here, he'd be extended the same vagabond privileges Cade enjoyed. As far as he knew, Morris hadn't done anything to get those revoked—yet. And if Cade was completely unlucky, any suit would go in front of Torsten. The old ones stuck together, especially against fledglings who'd tried to kill their masters. It went against the order of things. It was dangerous. Torsten would almost certainly side with Morris.

Cade needed proof of wrongdoing. Something ironclad. And he needed it fast.

He hurried away from the cemetery, thoughts racing. *He's got to be using a bounty hunter.*

The old fuck was either too weak to take Cade himself, planning something more, or both. That comment about guessing Cade would stay in town was sinister. Had Morris had intended the attack to be a surprise but gotten over-eager? Missed a shift in the wind and was now trying something more aggressive? If he was on Plan B, did that give Cade an advantage? Or was that just what he wanted Cade to think?

Lya. He'll go after Lya.

Morris had scented her, seen her with Cade somewhere. Morris didn't just want him—he wanted both of them. That thought consumed Cade as he made his way home, taking a roundabout way out of the vain idea that any bounty hunters on his tail might not know where he was yet.

He couldn't put Lya in danger. Not for a fully justified but ill-conceived past misdeed he'd completely and utterly botched. She might be a warrior and fit as a fiddle, but Morris had pirated the Americas for centuries. He'd hidden gold, gems, and other valuables everywhere along the coast, which meant he could afford to hire the best, despite Cade raiding some of those stashes himself. He'd hire someone dangerous. Someone Cade wouldn't see coming.

For a fleeting moment, he considered simply leaving town. He needed no one's permission to go, only to enter the territory and stay as an unaffiliated vampire. He could just run. Pack up his few tangible valuables right now and leave for St. Augustine, where he had an old house. It was far enough away from Miami that Salvador and Luz wouldn't bother him, busy with tourists to drink from, and somewhere Morris would be reluctant to follow. All the sun in Florida would pain him more than usual in his current state. Maybe even kill him. Besides, it'd been ages since Cade had seen the ocean. He might've had some bad times at sea, but it had been his first love. Maybe it was time to get reacquainted.

And leave Lya behind?

She'd be fine. She was clearly a capable being, or she wouldn't be so far from home and daring enough to sleep with him. As long as she stayed away from Raleigh, she'd be safe, and if she did come back after he'd gone, Maria's claim would protect her.

As he dashed up the stairs to his apartment and locked the door behind him, he wrestled the idea of leaving her behind.

Morris wouldn't be that hard to kill if he went after her. Cade would do it himself, except that Morris's glamour wasn't any weaker, Cade had already royally fucked up in the first attempt, and a second would nullify any plea he might make that it'd been an accident if he got caught.

He dragged out the one large suitcase he kept. Evaluated the things he'd somehow managed to accumulate in almost two years in one place. Where had all this shit come from? All these clothes? The sleeve of a dress shirt crumpled under his grip, and Cade let it go. He wasn't mad at his belongings.

It was his own cowardice that had his borrowed blood pounding in his veins, his lips curled back in the grimace that signaled he was ready to strike.

He was thinking of *running away*. The unworthiness of it made him burn with shame as much as anger. He had something good here. Had met some*one* good. Someone who excited and thrilled him. Someone special. And he was going to run south, abandon all this, abandon *her*, because his past mistakes had caught up to him? He was going to leave Lya vulnerable because he was scared, when she didn't even know someone might be coming for her to get to him?

No. He'd stay. He'd find a way to fight Morris off, and whatever little bounty hunters might come for him. He hadn't lived nearly five hundred fucking years to be chased from his claims like a gull shooed off a fresh catch. He'd been a goddamn pirate.

It was time to remember how to fight like one.

Chapter 13: Lya

I swiped the shower fog from the bathroom mirror and tried to figure out if I'd ever been so fucked in my life.

It wasn't even the good kind of fucked, the kind I'd been anticipating all Goddess-burning day. It was the rough, soul-destroying kind. The kind I'd dealt with when the Lyon Conclave had told me that no, I couldn't love who I loved and, for the crime of doing so, I'd be exiled. That I should thank the bitch queens for the privilege, since it meant keeping my life.

I felt boxed in again. Trapped. My options were limited by the obligations I owed and had agreed to. Had that hag Callista known I was fucking Cade? Was this a setup? Or bad luck?

It didn't matter. Either way, the result was the same.

My phone chirped with a text message, and I flinched before recognizing it wasn't the tone I'd set for Cade. Then grimaced when I realized it was the one for Callista. Wrapped in my towel, I went out and snagged the phone from the counter.

Did you get the bounty notice?

I briefly considered playing the fool before shaking my head. There was no fucking with Callista. Not if I wanted to keep my life.

I swiped a message back. *The vamp? 500? Yeah.*

The client just sent over an addendum. Additional $100k if delivered within 3 days.

I stared at the phone. These figures were outrageous. I mean, so was the risk, but what the fuck had Cade done to have someone throwing this kind of money around? Who had I been fucking? And who was the bloody client?

Not a question I could ask Callista. *Copy. Already working on it. Excellent. Keep me posted.*

"Sure," I muttered. "You and Cade both. That'll go over real well."

Being angry with Cade's threat had let me push aside the gut-deep twist of guilt at the way I'd left him. Now I had nobody left to be angry with except myself. Yeah, it sucked for him to have caught me like that. But he'd been acting within his rights as an Othersider, and maybe worse, he'd been dead-on with his reasoning, even without knowing it. The fact that I knew and had still left him hating himself on his bedroom floor only made me feel worse.

My stomach churned as I swapped the towel for pajamas and threw myself on my bed. I had a choice to make. One I already resented having put on me.

Me. Or him? My freedom. Or his?

It wasn't about doing the right thing because that was a matter of perspective. I would be harmed if I didn't look out for myself. He would be harmed if I didn't look out for him. Either way, someone was hurt, and in Otherside, I was the more vulnerable party. The smart, correct choice would have been to simply lure him out, take him down, and bring him in.

So why couldn't I bring myself to do it?

It'd be so easy. Pick up the phone. Call him. A little sweet talk, a little apology for reacting the way I had. He was clearly into me.

My hand clenched around the phone, and I set it aside. I needed to sleep on this. Everything would be clearer in the morning, when the memory of Cade's hands on my body and his lips on mine wasn't so fresh.

When I wasn't quite so haunted by the despair in his gaze as he looked up at me, asking my pardon.

***

Dawn didn't bring any answers, nor did it deliver any messages from Cade. I tried not to let myself believe I deserved that as I trudged into work ten minutes early, just to give Farand one less thing to snipe at me about.

This morning was the complete inverse of yesterday. Rather than being filled with hope and excitement, I wrestled with dread and yet more guilt. Farand made some petty little comment that I ignored. Or, more accurately, didn't hear because he was so far beneath my notice that I couldn't even pretend to play the game.

As I slogged through paperwork, I told myself this would be in the past soon. I'd have a new life. I just had to buy it with Cade's blood.

Nope. That didn't sit well at all.

My phone buzzed with a message while I was waiting for my lunch at the Thai place on Main. I made myself remember to breathe as I fished it out, my heart beating faster as I hoped it was Cade as much as I feared it was Callista.

It was Shonda, asking if I wanted to join another girls' night.

After chewing my lip, I grimaced and swiped a reply. *Can't. Big thing came up at work that's gonna have me pulling late ones. Raincheck?*

Big thing at work, or big thing in the sheets? What happened with tall, dark, and rich?

I snorted and looked up to find the hostess approaching with my lunch. I took advantage of collecting it and crossing the street

118

to the tables in Five Points Plaza to give myself a minute to think.

Could I talk to Shonda? I felt like a taker, not like a real friend. But she'd asked. Sometimes it was hard to tell with Americans, especially in the South—plenty of times they asked to be polite, rather than because they wanted to know the answer. Maybe sharing something was how I could make a friend though?

With a huff as much for the situation as to blow on the food, I picked a red bell pepper out of the basil sauce then another, until all that was left was the double order of chicken.

Definitely work, I wrote back, a*nd I'm not sure about my new friend.* I jittered, picking out and eating the juicy chunks of chicken as I waited for her response.

Girl what happened? You okay?

At that, I was biting my lip again, this time not to cry. Maybe she really did care and I'd been keeping her—and anyone else who might have become a friend—at arm's length. Was I really that scared of being burned again? Obviously yes, if an unexpected yet simple kindness had me three different kinds of emotional.

I'm fine. He's maybe just not who I thought he was.

Did he hurt you?

No.

Well. Not technically. Last night could have ended very badly, but now that I was out of the situation, I had to admit to myself that Cade had still handled it with excellent self-control and I'd only really been mad because he'd caught me.

Which just made it harder to believe he would have done something that merited a bounty at all, let alone one of the size on him.

I just think he's hiding something.

He looked rich as hell. Probably rich man shit. Like a wife or somethin.

I laughed out loud at that. A vampire? Married? They weren't elves, or even weres, who obsessed about their bloodlines and breeding up more of themselves. *You're probably right. How's Nicole? How are you?*

Shonda filled the rest of my lunch break with outrageous office gossip and disparaging comments about men in general. My heart eased at first, at the idea of finally making a friend.

But then I had to turn my feet back to the office, back to Farand and the thought in the back of my head that the bounty hadn't said what Cade was wanted *for*, only that he was presumed armed and dangerous.

Okay, so maybe that meant he'd hurt someone. Either he'd killed that someone and their people were seeking blood for blood, or he hadn't and they were seeking vengeance for themselves. Or maybe he'd stolen something?

My brain conjured a million reasons why he might deserve this. They swirled through my head as I did the petty paperwork Farand could have done himself but stacked in my inbox then did the research to prep for the next day's bail bond runs.

By the time the day ended, I had a splitting headache squeezing in a band around my head.

I couldn't keep doing this. I'd never second-guessed a bounty before. I wouldn't be second-guessing this one now if I hadn't fucked the man twice—and if I wasn't still hot for a third time, despite everything. I couldn't even tell myself off for mixing business with pleasure because I hadn't known Cade would be business when we'd met. I'd just known he'd treated me with respect and obeyed my boundaries to the letter.

But at the end of the day, none of that would save me from Callista, let alone the queens back in Lyon.

Fuck. I couldn't see a way out of this.

I'd given my word to Callista. The local queens, Torsten, and the joint werecat pride might have a power-sharing agreement that kept the peace, but Callista was the head bitch in charge. She'd have told her client she had someone on it. Backing out would cost her, which meant it'd come out of my hide. Probably quite literally, given the rumors of a torture dungeon in the basement of her damn bar. I was stuck.

I didn't do stuck.

As that thought settled over me, so did calm. I'd do what I had to do. Cade would do what he had to do. And that was that.

I spent the rest of the evening doing research. Most of the hard shit was done. I already knew where he lived. I knew the layout of the apartment. I'd noted the general security measures and could easily bypass them, either with mundane skills or my relatively weak control of Aether. I had an idea of Cade's habits and had seen what he was like at midmorning, when he was tired and slowed by the daylight and spent energy. That was the general idea sorted.

There were a few risks.

He might have someone at his apartment with him. Doubtful—I hadn't caught any scents there other than his, mundane or Othersider. From what little I knew of vampire culture, vagabonds tended to live a highly solitary life, which would play in my favor.

Risk two: he might not be as slow and sluggish as I expected if he hadn't spent the night expending energy on one-night stands.

Risk three: he was only acting the gentleman in a long game to win me over for blood and was in fact the kind of man who would hurt or kill me if I fucked this up.

Something about that didn't feel right though. If he was only after my blood, he could have taken it last night. He'd let me go. I grimaced as that started doubt cascading through me again, so I forced the thought aside.

I didn't have room for doubt or concern or questions. Only the job.

Next question: how soon to go. I had to be fast. Cade had said he doubted his safety. He knew someone was onto him. I'd already lost a day wallowing in emotions, a day he might well have spent fortifying his nest or outright moving. Maybe leaving town. Tonight would be unwise. I wasn't about to face a vampire in his own lair at night, especially not this close to a full moon, when my own Aetheric magic would be at its lowest ebb.

But tomorrow, noon? That could work.

I'd have to call in sick, and Farand would be beyond furious, given that I was supposed to be doing runs tomorrow. I wrestled with that for a bit, stomach clenching and sloshing with bile. One way or another, he would make me pay for making his life difficult.

Fuck him.

If I succeeded at this, Callista would free me from having to worry about that bastard ever again. I could take my money and get the hell out, far away from the Monteagues and everyone else associated with House Desmarais. If I failed, I wouldn't be worrying about anything again because, between Cade and Callista, I'd rather be drained than be taken by Callista's Watchers or the Darkwatch.

Fine. So I'd call in sick.

I had the when and where. Now the how.

Fortunately, that was the easiest part of the plan. If mundanes ever had cause to search my place, I'd be hauled up on several different weapons charges—assuming I didn't manage to mindmaze them with Aether and slip away. I couldn't manage a full-on maze, but I could do a little confusion spell. Ideally though, the police would never have a reason to come calling and find out what I had in my closet.

As I laid out the various weapons that could deal with vampires, I tried not to think of nights between Cade's sheets.

Stakes, check. Custom CUB knives and Cold Steel tantos, all with silver edges, check. Walther PPK thirty-two for my purse, check. Beretta nine-mil, check. Silver bullets for both. The Benelli M4 I'd leave at home, but the Gator Sawback was going in the car just in case.

A pang tightened my chest at that one. The only "just in case" that called for a machete on a vampire hunt was beheading. Stakes and silver were nonlethal. They'd paralyze or poison and give me room to work—and getting a grown man from his building to my car was definitely going to be work—but they wouldn't kill him.

I sat there in the middle of my living room, a mini arsenal laid out across the floor, and hated myself for what I had to do to survive, even as I prayed it'd be enough to pay off all my debts.

Chapter 14: Lya

I was already awake at dawn. Restless sleep had me haggard and cranky enough to actually feel ill. Or maybe that was just the prospect of a hunt I still didn't quite believe in. Either way, I sounded suitably and realistically shitty when I called in sick. Farand was equally shitty in his response. I mumbled something about food poisoning and put the phone down on him, not in the mood to put up with disparagement and abuse today.

As midday drew closer, I geared up and headed down to Raleigh. I managed to find street parking around the corner from Cade's apartment building, which I prayed meant the rest of the hunt would be as smooth—or as lucky. After checking all the weapons I carried were still concealed and my lockpick kit was in my purse, I tugged my cap down low, pulled the denim jacket hiding my snake tattoo closer, and got out. My heart hammered in my throat as I slipped in behind a resident and jogged up the stairs, taking them two at a time. There was nobody in the corridor outside Cade's unit, and I counted my blessings yet again.

The lock picked more easily than I thought it would. I slipped inside and gave my eyes a moment to adjust, not surprised to find the flat dark. That was the whole point of coming in the day—that Cade would be asleep and vulnerable.

I swallowed down the bile of guilt that bit at me.

Vulnerable. I was hunting a man I genuinely liked while he slept to serve my own ends. A man who, as far as I could tell, trusted me. Liked me back. Had treated me with nothing but respect and dignity.

As I hesitated, wrestling yet again with what I was doing, the air in the room shifted with movement right before someone slammed into me from behind and locked their arms around me. From the iron-and-ash scent of vampires blended with Cade's personal granite scent, I was deeply fucked.

He wasn't asleep. He'd been waiting for someone to come for him. Tipped off? Or still paranoid?

My arms were pinned to my sides. Then, just as quickly as my assailant had struck, he melted away. I spun, drew one of my silver-edged tantos, and crouched in a combat stance to face a completely shocked Cade.

My brain picked up useless details: he was dressed in grey sweatpants and a white T-shirt I'd never imagined him wearing after all the three-piece suits and designer jeans. He must have had a beard when he'd died, because his normally clean-shaven face was stubbled, and it was sexy as hell.

His clockwork motions said he hadn't fed yet today. "Lya? What the fuck is this?"

I almost flinched at the betrayal in his voice. Almost. But I had a job to do and no room for sentimentality. All my earlier doubt was gone, washed away under a burst of adrenaline. "I'm sorry. I have to."

His eyes narrowed. "Who put you up to it?"

"Does it matter?" I lunged and slashed with the blade, falling back when Cade dodged, made a grab for my wrist, and missed. Good to know a half-elf might be fast enough to down an exhausted vampire.

125

"Yes, it matters." His face tightened with frustration. "You can tell yourself this is just a casual thing however much you want, but I saw your expression the other night."

I snarled and pushed away the memory that tried to rise up. "It *doesn't matter.*"

"It does." He tried to catch my gaze.

"Not when I have debts to pay. I don't want to hurt you, Cade, but I can't afford to let you go."

"It's like that?"

I didn't bother to answer, darting in and trying again to land a strike. Garlic and crosses didn't do shit against a vampire, but the silver edging my blade was a poison that would give me room to figure out what the hell to do with all the emotions he was dredging up. A stake through the heart would paralyze him, but he could conceivably recover during transport, not to mention it'd be difficult to hide as I carried him out, doubly so if I had to maze a human. I didn't think I could bring myself to behead him, regardless of the Sawback in the back of my Ford Escape. But Callista had me over a barrel with this job, and I had to do what was best for me: get it done.

His next move was way too fast. I should have known he'd only been playing tired. Or maybe he just decided to take me seriously.

I dodged then dodged again and slashed ineffectively as he tried to grab me. His third attempt succeeded. The tug on the wrist of my knife hand nearly took my shoulder out of joint, and we crashed to the floor as I dug in my feet, drew on Aether, and tried to lever away.

"Hekate burn it, Lya." Cade used his greater body weight to his advantage, pinning me to the floor on my back and closing his fingers around my throat before I could voice a spell. With his other hand, he slammed my wrist into the floor until the knife spun from my numb fingers. "I don't want to hurt you, but I won't let you kill me."

I used all my training trying to throw him off. Didn't work. Black spots crept in at the edges of my vision as I gasped for breath, then took over entirely. The last thing I was aware of was his whisper.

"I'm sorry."

***

My shoulders were killing me when I woke up. I kept my eyes closed, pretending I was still out as I tried to determine what the hell my situation was. From the bloodless feeling of my hands and the roughness chafing my wrists, I was suspended by ropes. The smell said we were still at Cade's. The headache and tender spots on my body said I'd gotten my ass kicked.

"I know you're awake, Lya."

I blinked my eyes open to find my bare toes hovering an inch from the floor. "You took my shoes off?"

Possibly the least important question, but it's what popped out of my mouth.

"And your belt and searched you for more weapons." Cade sounded pissed, and I didn't blame him. "You're a walking bloody arsenal. Or rather, you were."

"Comes in handy. Usually."

"What do you usually hunt?"

I didn't see any harm in answering that, but I didn't.

His long, pale feet edged into my vision the moment before he gently tilted my head up then up again. "Take a good look at those ropes."

Wincing at the strain to my neck and shoulders, I obliged him, since I needed to know how to get out of them.

"Once upon a time, I was what they now call a privateer," he said coldly. "I never forgot how to tie a good knot. You're not getting loose unless I want you to."

From what I could see, I had no reason to doubt his confidence. It didn't stop me from twisting my wrists in frustrated defiance, cursing my luck for being tasked to bring in a vampire who'd started life as a Goddess-damned pirate.

Of course he had.

"Get it out of your system, love. We're going to be here until I get some answers." He released my chin.

I shook my head then let it hang, panting as much from my exertions as from the pain. "I can't. You know I can't."

"You can, and you will." He sighed. "Come on, Lya. You had plenty of chances to either tag me or come clean before now, which tells me this is something recent. What changed? Is it because of last night?"

The hint of guilt in his voice hit me like a punch to the gut. "No."

"Then what?"

"I only want my freedom," I snarled. I didn't want to feel for him, but I did, even as I hung there waiting for him to get tired of questioning me and just drain me. "You happen to be my ticket. That's all. It's not personal. I like you. A lot. But—"

"You have debts. You mentioned." He tilted his head, his motions all clockwork-jerky. "Only the powerful are free, Lya. You could use me to pay off this debt, but you'd still be in hock to whoever holds it until you were powerful enough to kill them. There's always one more job. One more debt. One more prize. One more life. Until yours is gone."

My guts froze, both at the bitterness of his words and the sharpness of his motion. We were in dangerous territory. My striking at midday meant he was weak from not feeding.

But his not feeding meant he'd be fighting his instincts—or giving into them. Elven blood was irresistible to some vampires. Even as I watched, his pupils dilated a little more. Not the sclera-black that'd say he was about to strike but far too wide for my comfort.

Shit.

"What about that scared you?" he asked, whisper-quiet.

"That it's true." Honesty spilled from my lips before I could wall it behind stubbornness. "But mostly that you look like a vamp who might be hungry."

"Oh, I am. You knew I would be at this time of day. You came anyway. Eat-or-be-eaten says I drain you, love."

A breath he didn't need to take hissed between his teeth as adrenaline spiked in me and sent my heart racing even faster.

He was right, and by Otherside laws, within his legal rights as well. I'd attacked him and lost. Unlike mundane bail bonding, bounties in Otherside weren't legally binding. There was no jurisdictional force outside any one faction's leaders and territories. Strength backed them up.

Callista had issued the bounty, but if she didn't give a shit about me, there'd be no vengeance, let alone rescue—and I knew she didn't, especially if I couldn't pull this off. I was disposable. That was why I'd been sent. I could tell myself it was my unique skills and situation all I liked, but deep down I knew the real reason. I was desperate, and I didn't matter to anyone on this side of the ocean—or in Lyon, for that matter. For all I knew, the entire situation had been an elaborate setup to get rid of me and end the shaming of my mother's House.

Cade inhaled like he was evaluating my scent this time. "I take it you're reconsidering your situation?"

"Always do." I gritted my teeth, furious with myself for getting caught. Everything had been way too easy right up until

129

it went to hell. Now I was strung up and waiting for slaughter unless I could change his mind.

"Not very well, it seems."

I didn't answer, looking anywhere but his eyes as I tried to figure out how to get out of this. I refused to just curl up and die. Not for the Lyon Conclave, not for the Chapel Hill Conclave, and not for Callista.

Whatever larger game was going on here, I'd play my way out of it, no matter what.

Cade was the fulcrum between the two sides, but I didn't know which way he'd tilt now. All I knew was that he'd been a gentleman in each of our encounters, including this one. So far, at least. Never a slip. That told me he was patient enough to outlast me here. Given the pain pinching my shoulders, I'd have to give in soon, if only to ensure I'd continue to have the use of my arms.

He eased closer, head tilted again like he was considering me. "What if I helped you?"

Pulled out of my situational calculus, I frowned and almost forgot not to look him in the eye. "What?"

"Tell me who's after me. I help you kill them instead. Then we'll both be free."

The idea of someone managing to kill Callista made me laugh. I tried to stop, but a blend of incredulity and despair made me keep going until tears rolled down my face.

Cade tilted my head up again. "You really don't think we can beat them?"

This time, I was too distracted not to meet his eyes. "Would I be here if I did?"

His gaze searched mine. "I'd like to think not. But apparently I don't know you as well as I thought I did."

Tilting my head to the side, he breathed deep at my neck. I shuddered as his fingers pinched on my chin and his teeth grazed the skin over the spot in my neck where veins and arteries were most closely bundled together.

Then he released me and backed up a few steps. "No. I said you'd beg but not like this." A crooked smile tilted one side of his mouth upward. "Hang tight."

He was gone before I could come up with a reply.

Chapter 15: Cade

Cade fled from his nest, distraught enough by the situation with Lya not only to leave her hanging from his bedroom ceiling but also to go out in broad daylight without sunscreen or sunglasses. He had to get out of that room, away from the irresistible woman strung up with all her pulse points exposed. He still had his emergency stash of bagged blood in his closet to tide him over, fortunately, or even his iron grip on his instincts wouldn't save her from him.

She smelled too good. He wanted her too much. He *cared* about her too much, even if he had to pretend not to, as much to himself as to her, to leave her suspended in a way that he could tell was already paining her. She was tough though, and determined, which meant he was truly in danger if he showed enough mercy to let her down.

He fucking hated it.

Lya didn't just practice martial arts for exercise or self-defense. She was a fucking bounty hunter. Not only that but from the way she reacted to his proposal to kill whoever had the contract on him, she was in hock to Callista or to someone who owed Callista.

This had to be Morris's play. Lya probably didn't even know anything beyond the details of the bounty, which rarely included a reason. If this one did, she'd think him a monster. Which would be fair, he had been for a time, but wasn't now. Or he tried not to be, not anymore.

Of all the fucking luck. Cade was confident he could've killed just about anyone in the Triangle, short of one of the faction heads or Callista herself. That hag hadn't given a damn about him the entire time he'd been here. There weren't many people who gave enough of a shit about Cade or knew enough about him to want him captured or dead. He was beneath Torsten's notice, unless someone had told the master vampire about Cade trying to burn his own master to death. Maria seemed to like him, and he had an understanding with Aron. The only other *moroi* he'd interacted with were Maria's people, and they'd all seemed to like him well enough too.

Morris was the only answer that made sense.

He'd known Morris was rich but rich enough to tempt Callista? He must have had treasure caches that even Cade hadn't known about, or had offered her something worth even more to her than gold from one of the remaining ones. He must have bought off Torsten as well, unless he either didn't know or the power-sharing agreement in the area was so solid that the Viking bastard would let a fellow *moroi* be hunted to maintain it. Vagabond guest rights should have at least gotten him a warning in that case.

But no. It had been just his luck that he'd fallen asleep on the couch rather than torture himself with Lya's scent in his bed, which was the only reason he'd heard the lock click open and been able to get the drop on her.

What a fucking mess.

Keeping to the shade thrown by the buildings, Cade made his way to a pop-up stand that sold quick food—burgers, sandwiches, fries—and ordered a double burger and fries. He had no idea what he was going to do with Lya yet, but she'd need something to keep her strength up. Either to fight him or be drained by him.

Cade shuddered at the idea of taking her last blood, fighting down the instinctive desires that whispered to him. He was more than that. At least, that's what he told himself the whole way home, eyes darting for the backup she'd have brought if she was smart and spotting no one. They were either good enough not to be seen, or Lya was that good—or that isolated.

A pained, halting, gasping sound caught his ear as he stormed back into his apartment and slammed the door.

Lya, struggling to breathe. He dropped the bag of food on the table and dashed to the bedroom, afraid of what he'd find.

The woman had somehow managed to wrench the eyebolt free from the ceiling and had knocked the wind out of herself when she landed on the floor, dislocating one of her shoulders for good measure.

Downed, struggling prey should have sent Cade over the edge, but something fluttered in his chest. Not his heart—it was barely beating—but something emotional.

Something he definitely didn't have time for right now but which called almost as seductively as her blood did. Shoving it aside, he stalked toward her, catching her easily when she tried to wriggle away.

"I don't know where the fuck you imagined you'd go. You have to know I can track your scent." Annoyance with himself and this whole Hekate-damned situation made his voice harsher than he'd meant it to be as he hoisted her upright, mindful of her arm, and marched her into the dining room. At the table, he pushed her to drop into a chair and straightened her as she finally caught her breath. "Don't move."

Before she could protest, he gripped her left shoulder with one hand and her arm with another, carefully pulled with a slight twist, and pretended it didn't wrench something inside him to hear her bite back a cry of pain as her shoulder popped back into joint.

They stared at each other while she steadied her breathing. She carefully avoided meeting his gaze directly, but she didn't so much as glance at the food. Cade tilted his head back, inhaled slowly, and let it out even slower as he brought himself down from a surge of hunger that twisted his stomach and made him salivate.

Lya didn't move, a snake watching an eagle.

Her small flinch when he looked at her again irritated him. He'd done nothing—

Well, he'd taken her by the throat the other night and accused her of preparing to do exactly this then choked her out and hung her from the ceiling just now. Which just irritated him further because they'd both been right.

Neither of them was technically in the wrong with Otherside's labyrinthine system of rules and obligations, so it'd have to be worked out between them.

"Eat," he snapped as he fetched one of her knives from the kitchen counter. She held stock-still as he cut the ropes binding her wrists together. "Or don't. But don't go anywhere. We need to talk."

When Lya cautiously reached for a fry, he headed for his blood stash in the bedroom closet. *Hell of a second date.*

He half expected her to be gone when he came back with a chilled bag of A-positive, but she was chewing the burger with the mechanical motions and blank stare of someone who'd either resigned themselves to death or was actively hating themselves.

In her case, maybe both. She didn't react as he heated some water on the stove and dropped the bag in.

"I tried to kill my master," Cade said softly.

She jumped and started coughing when a bite went down the wrong way.

He waited for her to recover before he continued. "Thought I had, rather. Morris was a bastard. The worst sort. Vampires shouldn't survive long at sea—there's too much sun and not enough food. But he captained my ship. You can imagine how vicious he was with captives."

Lya put down her food and shifted to face him, blank-faced and still not speaking. Somehow, it was harder to talk with her full attention on him, and he turned back to the warming blood, using the tubes sticking out of the bag to lift it enough to see if it was ready. Not quite.

"Did you know we live longer and can tolerate sun better when we feed on Othersiders?" he asked. "Other vampires included."

"No." It was the first word she'd said since he'd gotten back. He took it as progress, especially when she continued in a halting voice. "I thought you just liked the power in the blood. Like...like it made you drunk or something."

"Oh, it does. Even gives us a hangover if it's strong enough. But it's the regenerative properties that make us covet it." He'd be killed for telling her this. These were secrets long and closely held among the *moroi*. He couldn't make himself care. "Morris turned me at the end of my first tour on his ship. Said I was too pretty to pass up and he needed someone to keep him youthful with all the damn Caribbean sun."

Cade checked the blood again. It was ready. He clicked off the stove, dumped the water, and slid into the chair across from Lya.

When she stared at the bag, brows lifted, he said, "Would you rather be the donor this fine afternoon?"

He'd expected a quick, repulsed no.

She just swallowed hard and went sallow, as though she was seriously considering it.

"Eat your food," he prompted before he could be distracted by the idea of sinking fang. When she returned to her wooden bite-chew-swallow, he picked up the thread of his story. "Some master vampires treat their fledglings reasonably well or even love them. From what I've seen, Maria treats hers exceptionally well, and Torsten's abuse seems restrained to gaslighting and denial of opportunity. Morris...he liked to hurt people. Physically and otherwise. Especially his fledglings. I'm the only one who survived him, assuming he was telling the truth when he described how he tortured all the ones before me to death."

Lya put the burger down again, looking like she was going to be sick. "How long?"

"Two hundred years. Until I staked him and burned him alive."

She swayed and bent over her knees, breathing in fast, shallow gulps like she was about to be sick, and Cade took a minute to drink some of the blood. It flooded into his system like a balm, nowhere near as soothing as drinking from Lya would have been but far more tolerable for his psyche.

"Problem is, I didn't kill him. I thought I had. He was burned beyond any recognition. Humans were coming though, so I ran."

"He recovered?" she asked the floor.

"Yes and has apparently been following me from city to city for some part of the last two hundred and ninety-six years, keeping tabs on me as he regained strength and sought an opportunity. One he found here in Raleigh, where the local vampires are hobbled by a power-sharing agreement with the elves and the weres and all of them are headed by a ruthless bitch of an Arbiter with a thirst for more power and a bone to pick with parties unknown."

He finished the bag of blood while Lya processed that and got herself under control, squeezing the bottom and rolling his fingers up to push every last drop up to the tube he was using as a straw.

She looked haunted when she straightened. "There was no reason given on the bounty. I figured it had to be bad, but I didn't know anything."

That sparked something darkly furious in him. "And you took it anyway? Without asking me?"

His tone must have pinched her guilt, because she glared at him. "You're a five-hundred-year-old predator with a five-hundred-thousand-dollar bounty on your fucking head! You think I'm gonna roll over in post-coital bliss and say, 'Hey babe, you want to tell me about this dark past you must have since someone's just hired me to bring you in incapacitated?' Goddess save me."

The blood in Cade's belly curdled, and everything else she'd said flew in one ear and out the other. "He wants me alive?"

"Assuming it's this Morris who contracted the bounty, yes."

"What the hell kind of debt are you carrying that you'd do this?" He hadn't realized he'd voiced the thought aloud until Lya wilted, her jaw still clenched in what smelled like a blend of stubbornness and shame. "Love, who's holding your freedom?"

She jerked then shoved the rest of the burger in her mouth, followed by a few fries, looking less like she had an appetite and more like she was buying herself time. "House Monteague, on behalf of my mother's House. Over them, Callista. I'd already promised her I'd do the job before I knew you were the target or that it was even a vampire hunt she was hiring for. Blank check in exchange for getting me free of my exile and a fat payday to start my new life. Like I said, it wasn't personal. And I…I'm sorry. I should have said something. But I couldn't find a way, and for a bounty that big, I figured you had to have done something pretty fucking bad and that maybe you were just toying with me. For blood."

Cade sighed, scrubbing a hand over his face and through his hair as though it could dislodge the exhausted frustration. "That's fair."

"It is?"

He shrugged. "I am what I am. You are what you are. We're both trying to get by in a system that has fucked us. But I meant what I said before."

"That you'd be a fool not to hunt me?"

"No. Well, yes, but not that. That whatever you need, I can give you. Or I'll find a way."

"Why?" she whispered. Tears filled her eyes and threatened to fall as she blinked them away. "I just came after you. I would have—"

"Doesn't matter. You didn't, and if you had…well, I'm a vampire who tried to kill his master. I had it coming." He couldn't keep the bitterness out of his voice. He'd been so close to having everything, and now Lya would probably—

No, he wouldn't let himself assume what she'd do. They'd both done that, and look where it'd gotten them.

Silence stretched until she broke it. "My family and my lover stood by and watched as the Conclave of Lyon sentenced me to exile."

Cade looked at her sharply enough that she jumped.

After a quick swallow and a sip of water, she continued, her tone dead and her words stilted. "Henri is a prince. A lesser branch of the House, but still elven fucking royalty. I'm half-human. No matter how royal my own mum is, I'm not. I had no business loving him. Or him me. But we did. Love each other. Only, his mother, the new bloody House queen, didn't think I was good enough. They needed to set an example." When she looked at him, defiance sparked as she met his gaze for the first time all day. "Nobody spoke for me. Nobody wanted me enough. Nobody *loved* me enough. They were *supposed* to care about me. But I'm trash, and now I'm in exile. So why the fuck would you do anything for me if it's not for blood?"

The tears that had glistened broke free as sudden fury twisted her face, twin trails racing down her face before she scrubbed them away.

"What do you want with me, Cade?" Her tone was heated.

All he could do was stare. This brilliant, capable, fierce, beautiful woman thought herself unlovable? Undesirable? Unworthy? His mind realigned as he processed what she'd said. This wasn't about him or anything he'd done.

It was her. As broken and afraid to care about someone as he was.

"What?" She stood so quickly the heavy chair toppled backward.

When he still didn't respond, she started clawing at the rope still knotted around her wrists, growing increasingly agitated as the knots refused to give.

Cade ghosted from his seat to stand in front of her.

Lya watched him warily, panting and sweating as he slowly reached first for her right hand then for the knife still on the table.

He cut through each binding with the utmost care. If he slipped and broke her skin, he didn't think he'd be able to rein himself in. Not with her scent spiking through his apartment, making the blood he'd just drunk pulse in him, throbbing with twin needs.

She darted away when the last rope slipped free, rubbing her wrists and glaring at him with bone-deep suspicion. "What is this?"

"I told you. Anything I can give you."

The part of him that had driven him to survive for nearly five hundred years raged against this. The part of him that still clung to hope and decency shut it down as the part that was just so tired of it all washed over him.

He held his arms out, wrists together for her to bind him as he'd bound her. "Apparently that's me."

The fury drained from her in a wash of shock. She flinched away. "No. I'm not taking you back to your abuser. I'm sure as shit not killing you to do it."

"Lya—"

"No!" She buried her face in her hands and shuddered. "No. Thank you. But I can't be that person. I can't be *this* person. Not anymore. I…I'm sorry. I don't deserve this. Or you."

She stepped closer, her brown eyes searching his face as she hesitantly pushed his hands down. It took everything in him to stay still when she clasped his jaw in both hands, leaned forward, and kissed him.

Cade reveled in it. The taste of her mouth and the salt of her tears, their dampness as her face pressed to his.

He fisted his hands, not wanting to scare her or tip the scales either way in whatever decision or declaration she was making with this kiss. He just wanted more. More her. More this. Even with the pain this afternoon had brought. After years of running from connection, the voice of survival in the back of his mind was quietly screaming at what he was doing.

When Lya pulled away, she looked even more vulnerable and confused than she had the other night. "I'll make this right."

"You don't owe me anything," he said. When she pressed her lips together and looked equal parts stubborn and regretful, he sighed and slumped. "If you're not going to take your bounty…"

"Yeah. I'll get out. Thank you. For everything. It's not enough, but it's all I have for now." She picked up her knife, and when he didn't protest, gathered everything else. Put her hat, shoes, and belt back on, tucked everything away, and slipped out with a last scared look.

Cade would have been frightened too if he had to face Callista emptyhanded. Which meant he was going to have to find a way to make sure Lya didn't have to.

Chapter 16: Lya

He'd let me go.

Cade had cut me loose, fed me lunch, and let me go.

No bites. No promises or oaths required. Just complete and utter dejection and disappointment.

I couldn't believe it, and yet here I was, back in my apartment, blood untouched, life intact. My shoulders still hurt like a bitch and my wrists were raw from the ropes, but he'd let me take back all my weapons, which would have been a major pain in the ass to replace. I almost wished he'd drained me. At least then I wouldn't have to live with feeling like the shittiest person on the planet or the gut-wrenching fear of having to face both Farand and Callista tomorrow.

What the fuck was I going to say, let alone do? I'd been rude to Farand this morning, so certain that one way or another I was getting out.

The one thing I did know was that I owed Cade more of an apology than I'd left him with. Something that would be expressed in action, not just words. But what could I offer him to make this right, other than blood?

Then it hit me like a sunrise: his sire and master. I could offer to hunt that asshole instead.

The idea rumbled around in my head while I put everything away, showered, and paid some bills. It'd be dangerous as hell but no less dangerous than what I'd already agreed to do for Callista. Cade had demonstrated that quite clearly.

I made mental notes of what I knew, not daring to write anything down. The sire's name was Morris. He'd been captain on Cade's ship, and to survive however many centuries as a vampire at sea meant he was a real brutal badass. But Cade had also burned him nearly to death. Close enough that he'd thought Morris *was* dead. That'd take ages to recover from without drinking from a full-blood Othersider every day, and he wouldn't have the strength to catch one or enough spare blood in him to turn a human and grow a new crop of fledglings.

I could take him. If Cade would accept my help.

I got a few more things done and cooked dinner while I waited for the sun to set. I had no idea if Cade would have gone back to bed or moved to a safer location, but waiting for nightfall would be polite. At least, that's what I told myself—that it was courtesy, not a hot blend of shame and fear that had me putting it off.

At sunset, I bit my lip and pulled up his number, tempted just to send a text. But this was big and dangerous in a way that had nothing to do with the hunt and everything to do with defying Callista and the so-called natural order of things. Resolutely, I stabbed my thumb down on the call button.

When it rang a bunch of times, I almost hung up.

But then Cade answered. "I wasn't expecting to hear from you again."

I flinched at the faint hint of accusation in his tone. "I owe you."

"I already told you—"

"Look, just let me do this, okay? I like you, Cade. I like you a hell of a lot, and I shouldn't because I know how it ends when I start to give a shit about someone. But I do, and I want to make shit right with you." I snapped my mouth shut at what I'd just admitted to myself as much as to him.

I did like him. This wasn't just about justice and honor and striking back against abusive fucks. It was because I genuinely liked him. I refused to say love. I'd only known the man for a few days. But we had an undeniable connection.

One I'd fucked up, maybe unforgivably so.

"Cade?" I said after a moment.

"What did you have in mind?" His neutral tone promised nothing.

But hope flared in my heart. "I kill Morris."

Silence. Then, "Excuse me?"

"We assume it's Morris who put the bounty on you, right? You said he's been following you around. So he has to be in town somewhere."

"He is. He's in Raleigh. I tracked him to City Cemetery, but I don't know that he's staying there. Lya, if killing him was an option, I'd have done it."

"Oh." I deflated a little. "Why isn't it an option?"

"The Détente?"

"That just says we can't get caught doing it by the mundanes. He'll have a lair or something, right?"

"He will, but I'm still not agreeing to this. He threatened you."

That sparked rage in me. "He what?"

"He must have been watching the night you came back to mine. He wants you. Not just your blood. He wants to hurt you. Like he did me. To get at me." Guilt tinged Cade's voice and under it, anger.

I paced the room in a fury. "That makes it personal. I didn't do shit to him."

"I know but…" He sighed. "But nothing. This is my fault. I got careless. Stayed in Raleigh too long. Lya, I don't want to see you harmed."

"I'm a bounty hunter. It's in the job description, and either way, I'm within my rights to defend myself. But I am asking that you let me fix things between us. An apology isn't enough."

"Why?"

I frowned. "Why what?"

"Why do you want to fix things? Why this way?"

"I told you. I like you."

"Like as in…"

"I don't know. Care." I hugged myself with my free arm as a spike of anxiety jabbed through my core then rushed to blurt out the rest. "I enjoyed our date. I like how I feel when I'm in your arms. Not just the sex. The after too. I want to see where this could go if we're not playing games."

"Oh." The note of surprised pleasure in that one little word eased me. "In that case, I'm coming with you. We'll hunt Morris together."

I started to tell him no, that this was my debt, and then stopped. The two of us would go round and round on debts and payments until the sun came up. Besides, I'd never hunted with a partner. It could be fun. At the very least, it'd be safer than trying to hunt a vamp as old as Morris had to be alone.

I did try to learn from past mistakes. Usually.

"Deal," I said. "Callista said yesterday there was an extra hundred grand tacked on for the job to be done in three days. That gives us two more days before she'll expect an update from me."

"Yesterday. After I saw him. He's scared. The old bastard is scared of *me*." Cade's grim satisfaction set my heart racing, and his dark chuckle sent it pacing even faster. "Good. Give me tonight to track him down."

146

"Okay." I couldn't help a silly grin, and I didn't even scold myself for it.

"Thank you for this, Lya. I'll be in touch. Take care of yourself until then. Don't let your cousins get under your skin, okay?"

I'd almost forgotten telling him about that. "Yeah. I'll try. Low profile."

"Exactly."

"Bye, Cade."

He said goodbye and hung up, leaving me with flutters of more than anticipation. If we could pull this off, we might both be able to free ourselves from our pasts. He wouldn't have the shade of his old master hanging over him. I could finally let go of what'd happened in Lyon and focus on making a new life here in the Triangle, rather than floating on the edge of Otherside society, feeling like a resentful, unwanted ghost. I'd still have to hold to the terms of my exile agreement, but maybe it'd be more palatable if I didn't feel quite so alone.

For the first time in ages, the prospect of the future excited me.

***

That excitement warped to dread the next morning. I literally kept my head down when I walked through the door of the agency, moving a little slower than usual in an effort to make it look like I really had been sick. Half-elves didn't get sick very often, but when we did, everyone knew it was bad. It had to be a pretty nasty virus to overcome the elven antibodies that protected us from most human diseases.

"Look who it is," Farand said in a faux-sweet voice, tossing brown bangs out of his face. "Our favorite halfling, back from her vacation. Feeling better?"

I gritted my teeth at the slur. *Be smart. Be. Smart.* "Well enough."

"Sure you don't need to take another day? I know how frail you low-bloods are." He sneered. "So much for hybrid vigor."

Heat raced through me, and I clenched my fists. Kept walking. Dropped my bag on my desk and started sorting through the paperwork stacked on it. There was no way all this had come in just yesterday.

This was more punishment—work Farand or the other elves in the office didn't want. Drudgery or shit that was just complicated. They acted like I was here to clean up after them when I had the highest success rate in the office for bringing people in *and* the lowest error rate on paperwork. I'd always excelled because it hadn't been an option not to, and instead of celebrating me for it, they heaped more on my back and told me to carry it even further.

I closed my eyes and took a deep breath, looking for calm.

It snapped when Farand said, "Hey, halfling bitch. Answer your betters when they speak to you."

Someone gasped. Even they couldn't believe the lack of decorum and the outright hostility. The others had all looked away over the last few months as Farand's "hazing" had continued long past any reasonable time and clearly showed itself as unmitigated rancor. Not that I'd ever expected them to speak up for the one half-elf in the office. That would have required courage. That would have required decency. And honor. And so many things they either lacked or were happy to sacrifice in order to keep the peace and maintain a status quo that kept elves comfortable and everyone else secondary.

Enough. I'd had enough and more than enough. My skin prickled as I wrestled down my small talent with Aether. Going head to head with him magically would be a mistake.

But words? I could use those.

"Goddess damn you, Farand." I couldn't keep the bitter snarl out of my words, even though I knew I'd pay for them. "Damn you and damn your House. I didn't ask for any of this. I didn't even do anything wrong, and yet all of you see fit to judge me."

I glared around the rest of the office so they'd know I was as sick of their silence as I was of Farand's voice. They were as guilty as he was because they let him think the treatment I'd received was okay.

"You all think you're *better* than me, and you know what? You're not. You never will be. That's why you're stuck here in this shitty little bail bond agency instead of working for the Darkwatch or as a political asset. Me? I could go anywhere. But you're *stuck*, and you're *nobody*, worse than me, because at least I was never expected to be anything other than a low-blooded mistake." My tirade left me panting and trembling with righteous anger. Everything I'd ever wanted to say to him for every little slight had come pouring out like pus from a lanced abscess.

In the ugly twist of Farand's mouth, the jut of his jaw, and the dangerous narrowing of his hazel eyes, I could see it was going to cost me.

"Are you done?" His words were a barely-there whisper. "Because you need to be. Before I have to remind you that some mistakes can be corrected."

The way he smiled then sent chills down my spine, like I'd just given him exactly what he was looking for. I tried to replay exactly what I'd said and couldn't, having been too hot in the moment to have any sense or calculation.

But I couldn't back down now. I wouldn't. I was done groveling and apologizing for doing nothing other than existing. I was done being considered less-than when I was greater than the sum of my heritage. With just scraping by on the limited dregs of the opportunities they saw fit to give me.

Bail bond runner? Fuck that. I could be an independent bounty hunter, a real one, on my own merit. I'd had my own independent gig in London. Callista's offer showed me I could have the same here. Working for Farand was just part of the punishment I'd been dealt.

I was done taking punishment I hadn't earned.

When I didn't answer him, Farand said, "Get out. Don't bother coming in tomorrow. You'd better pray that Callista takes you in because I'll see to it that the new terms of your exile have you shoveling pig shit in the boonies otherwise."

My guts clenched tighter than my jaw as I fought not to make this worse for myself.

I'd been right. But I hadn't been smart.

And now I definitely needed to get shit sorted out with Cade, Morris, and Callista, or I was more fucked than ever.

I grabbed my bag and backed up slowly, hands out to my sides, my attention not leaving Farand as I made my way out. I didn't quite run to my car, but I felt no shame in walking fast.

Chapter 17: Lya

Cade called as I was walking in my front door. "Morning, love. Good news. I've found him."

I tried to ignore the skip in my heart at the word "love." He'd said it before. I'd assumed he was just being British, but I was starting to think it was something else.

Either way, I had bigger issues. "Hey. I'm really glad to hear it because I need to get this hunt wrapped up quick."

He must have caught a note of something off in my tone because his voice dropped an octave. "What happened?"

"Um, you know how you said to try not to let my cousins get under my skin?"

"Shit. Are you safe?"

"I mean, for now. Farand sent me home though. Told me not to bother coming in again. Something about getting me sent east to shovel pig shit." I warmed with remembered fury at the confrontation. "I, ah, might have irreparably burned what was passing as a bridge."

"You're home now?"

"Yeah. Where's Morris?"

"Holed up in a house near the same graveyard where I encountered him before. The family living in it are all glamoured to hell and back, enough that it's a borderline violation of the Détente." Cade sighed, sounding tired and annoyed. "All right under Torsten's nose too, but neither Maria nor Aron knew anything about another vagabond in the area. They'll be furious if they have to pay the elves to have the Darkwatch do a coverup."

"Goddess." I thought through the ramifications quickly. "That means we could get away with an execution."

"Precisely. No record of entry, no permissions granted by the Master of the City or his second, the egregious glamouring, likely at least a few human deaths…the only thing that bothers me is whether Callista is aware of all this."

"I mean, he ran the bounty through her, and she has her damn Watchers. Assume she knows at least some of it. Plus, Morris has to know you're planning something yourself, since you haven't followed your usual pattern and left town."

"So we need to throw them off."

What would throw off the Watchers, Morris, and Farand all at once? Easy-peasy. "Hey—do you want to come over here and plan the hunt?"

He was silent for just long enough to make me nervous. Had I broken his trust too badly?

"I mean, if the daylight is an issue I can come to you. I just thought it'd be easier to plan in person."

"Daylight's not a problem. It's a risk to you for me to be there if Callista has Watchers on me. And I wasn't expecting to be invited to your home."

I winced. "I can be a little cagey."

He laughed. "You could be a vampire, love. But it won't be easy for Morris to follow me in the day. He's still too badly injured to withstand much sunlight. If you're comfortable with it, then yes, I'd love to see your home. And you." A growl entered his tone. "Maybe for more than planning? If that's okay with you."

It was my turn to laugh, although I had to swallow down a sob. *Somebody* wanted me. Valued me. Cared about me. Desired me. All of a sudden, the heat warming me wasn't rage.

I'd started the day reckless, might as well continue. "Yeah. Cost of admission is an orgasm."

"Well then. That's a price I'll happily pay. I need to get a few things ready here, but I'll come by later this afternoon. Sound good?"

I agreed then hung up and went about tidying the house in a flurry. There wasn't much to clean, but dishes needed to go in the dishwasher and the sheets could use a change. A bit useless maybe, given what I hoped to do in them. But they'd been on the bed a week, and while Cade might enjoy the extra scent, I had standards.

Next up was getting ready to go. Where, I didn't know. But I wasn't naive enough to think I could stay here, not without paying a price. One way or another, my life was about to change.

I could always unpack bags, but I couldn't unfuck myself. I'd pissed all over Farand earlier. Justified or not, I was supposed to be happy with being shat on and even though I'd only spoken the truth, there'd be repercussions. Farand had been clear on that. I hoped I could prove myself useful enough to Callista for her to bribe the queens to forget about a half-elf they didn't even want to acknowledge as existing anyway, but if I couldn't, I needed to be ready to skip town.

For better or worse, I didn't have much. My clothes fit in two suitcases, weapons in another. Personal effects in a shoulder bag.

With the house in order and my shit packed and ready to go, I poured myself a glass of orange juice and sat at the dining table to muse on a question that had popped into my mind as I put black sheets on my bed: whether I'd let Cade glamour and bite me at some point.

I enjoyed being glamoured. I didn't mind being bitten. I just hadn't known Cade well enough to feel comfortable with it, and we didn't have an arrangement like Maria and I had.

But he'd had me captive and strung up, ready to sample like a buffet, would have been within his rights to take what he wanted, given I'd attacked him first…and resisted. I'd seen him fight his instincts off. He had the control. I was trusting him to go on a hunt with me. One where I might well be injured.

Surely I could trust him to give us both a little more enjoyment?

A click at the front door pulled my attention. Frowning, I stood and peered down the hallway. The front door was unlocked when I was certain I'd locked it behind me when I came in. I always did. Then I was scrambling for the bedroom and the bag in which I'd just packed all my weapons, my body and instincts registering the threat before my mind could.

The door swung open, and the bells on it jangled as I skidded to a stop just shy of the hallway to the bedroom. There was a muttered "Make it quick," as two men burst into my apartment, guns with silencers drawn and pointed at the floor. They came up fast enough when the men spotted me.

The room flooded with the burnt marshmallow scent of elven Aether, much stronger than anything I was capable of.

Elves. Monteagues, from the dark hair and tawny skin of both of them, which meant this wasn't a Darkwatch mission. The Darkwatch used mixed triads, one member from each of the high Houses. This was personal, and if these two and their spotter outside were all Monteagues, they had to be Farand's friends.

"Stop," the foremost ordered in a hard voice. "Stand where you are."

I froze. The scar through his eyebrow gave him a competent cast I didn't dare fuck with. "What's this about? I haven't done anything."

He snorted as his companion took a step to the side to get a clear shot at me. "Maybe, maybe not. Frankly, I don't give a shit. I'm just here to pay off a debt."

"What debt?" My heart hammered in my chest because I suspected I knew the answer.

"You pissed someone off," the second elf said.

"How the fuck could I piss anyone off? I'm a fucking low-blood. I don't have enough power to—" The words stopped even as I was saying them because I realized what this was about.

It wasn't power or the lack thereof. It was that Farand felt like he'd lost face. I'd embarrassed him and the rest of the office when he was already out of favor. He must not have been able to get me fired like he'd threatened because I hadn't actually violated the terms of my exile.

But he could make sure I had an "accident."

Goddess, that was quick. I was expecting to have at least another day before having to deal with retaliation, had hoped that Cade and I could get the hunt done in that time.

I slowly raised my hands with the belated realization of how fucked I was. "Look, gents. Whatever Farand told you—"

"Oh good, you do know what this is about. Consider yourself served."

Without any further ado, both elves took aim. I tried to dodge into the living room as they fired. There was a *pop-pop*. Twin punches hit like a burst of fire. Then pain radiating from my thigh and flank.

I hit the floor before I could register what had happened. The bells on the door jangled again as they both slipped out.

"Shit." Pain flared as I forced myself to a sitting position and checked the damage.

A bullet was still lodged in my left thigh. Grimacing, I felt for an exit wound in my back and found one. Through and through, nearly missed me entirely. They'd been rushing and not aiming to kill, or I'd be dead. This was meant to be a punishment, a reminder Farand could take my life anytime he wanted to and would probably get away with it. A scare to get me to bow my head for real.

Fighting off the pain, I considered my options. Few and far between.

I couldn't go to a hospital. Not for gunshot wounds. There'd be a mundane police report. An investigation. It'd violate the Détente to draw human attention to Otherside matters, and then I'd be dead anyway. I had a first aid kit, but I'd be hard-pressed to use it, given that I'd likely pass out from the pain of digging in my own thigh for the bullet and I was about to find out what lead poisoning felt like.

It'd be a shame for my blood to go to waste, pooling on the carpet in slow ebbs. That made my choice easier. I forced myself to my feet and staggered back to the kitchen, where my phone was still on the bar counter. The blood on my fingers made it hard to unlock and dial, but I managed.

Cade picked up immediately. "Lya? Everything okay?"

A pang hit me, and I grunted, sliding to the floor before I could answer. "Hey. Dinner bell."

"What the hell are you saying?"

"Get it while it's hot," I panted, teeth clenched through another wave of pain. A human probably would have been fine. In a lot of pain but fine.

For better or worse, I wasn't fully human.

Lead was poisonous to elves, much like silver was to vamps and weres. I'd gotten a little more elf in my DNA than human, which meant that not only was I susceptible to slow-healing damage from lead-based weapons or ammo but also that the lead in the slug had started poisoning me as soon as it'd lodged in my body.

Poetic justice maybe, given that had been my plan for Cade.

"Where are you?"

If I didn't know any better, I'd think he was frantic. Who knew though? "Still at home. High-blood bastards picked my lock and let themselves in."

More poetic fucking justice.

"Are you alone? What happened?"

I laid all the way down on the floor, moving in small jerks until I found a position that didn't hurt as much—not that it helped the burning sensation of lead poisoning, which was hitting me far worse than the relatively minor bullet wounds. Cade was still talking, saying something about stay there, and I tried to laugh. Where the hell was I going to go like this?

All that came out was a pained cough.

"Stay on the phone," Cade's small voice ordered. "I'm on my way."

Maybe if he'd tried that tone in person, backed up by glamour, it would have worked. But I hung up and started crawling to the bathroom, where I kept a patch kit and Vitamin C tablets that would stave off at least a little of the damage. Chills shook me before I was halfway there, rattling me hard enough that I fell to the floor.

I had to get this bullet out, and I sure as hell wasn't going to wait for him to save me.

As I dragged myself into the bathroom, the inane thought that it was going to be a pain in the ass to get the blood out of the carpet made me snort.

More important concerns, Lya. Focus.

I made it to the bathroom. Pulled open the cabinet. Yanked out the big first aid kit then groaned when I realized all the glasses were still in the kitchen. The Vitamin C was an effervescent powder, something the mundanes marketed as cold and flu prevention. I needed to dissolve it in water, but the kitchen suddenly seemed a long way away as my teeth started chattering and my skin burned.

Get the bullet out.

I fumbled with the heavy tweezers I'd added to the kit for just this purpose, not having reckoned on how badly lead poisoning would affect me. I'd trained with substances. Not lead. The elves wouldn't handle the shit if they didn't have to, and I wasn't enough of a reason to have to.

My attempts to position the tips of the tweezers kept catching them on the edges of my wound, and I tilted my head back as my stomach rebelled at a particularly bad tear. I was damaging myself almost as much as the lead was. Didn't matter.

Grasping the damn tool in both hands, I tried again.

Chapter 18: Cade

If she's dead, I'll hunt every single one of them down and kill them.

The thought echoed through Cade's mind the entire ride over, and he was glad of the cap and sunglasses hiding what he was sure was a murderous expression. What the hell had Lya meant with the "dinner" comment?

When he arrived, he tried to keep his head down and his pace slow, even as he wanted to charge the door. The scent of elves was fading, so they'd probably simply come and gone rather than staying to harass Lya. He knocked twice then twice more as the Uber driver pulled away.

When there was no answer, he tried the doorknob.

The scent of blood, gunpowder, and elven Aether hit him like a cannonball as he let himself in amidst a clang of bells. He shut the door behind him and locked it, for all the good it would do if whoever had done this was tempted to come back.

She'd implied that she was injured, but he hadn't expected this. What the hell had happened today?

"Lya?" he called.

"In here." The unsteady but relieved response came from the hall on the left.

He followed the spots of blood on the carpet to a small, tidy bathroom pleasantly furnished in shades of green.

Lya was sprawled with her back against one door of an under-sink cabinet, the other door open and a first aid kit spilling supplies everywhere. A large pair of tweezers rattled against the floor with the force of the tremors shaking her, and Cade schooled his face to neutrality, not allowing his dismay at the state of her thigh show. From the torn-up wound and the bloody pliers, she was trying to dig something out. A bullet? Low odds with the tremors.

She tilted her head back and smiled weakly. "Hey."

"What needs help first?" He dropped his hat and sunglasses on the counter, shrugged out of his hoodie, and knelt, swallowing hard at the nearness of hot, powerful blood. Even half-elf was more Otherside than he'd taken in years, and from the smell of it, Lya leaned more toward elf than human. *Focus.* "Thigh?"

"Yeah. Bullet's still in." She offered the tweezers.

Cade caught them before they could hit the floor, and she shook her head as though to clear mental cobwebs, even as her teeth clattered.

"Lead poisoning is a bitch."

"I can see that."

As gently as he could, he braced his thumb and forefinger on either side of the wound in her thigh, which was slowly oozing blood. The skin around it was swollen and hotter than even a fever would account for, like the bullet was burning her from the inside.

She wavered, biting back a whimper at the light pressure of his hand, and the muscle under his fingers jumped.

"Glamour me," she said. "Please. Just a little. Before I throw up."

He looked up, shocked. "This wasn't what I had in mind when I said you'd beg."

"Shut up and do it, or we'll be here all day."

"When you ask so nicely…" He smiled at her small scowl, the amusement fading as she grimaced in pain again.

Cupping her jaw with one hand, he eased his grip on the magic. It leaped forward, fueled by the scent of blood, and he took it down a notch then down again as he reminded himself her elven heritage might make her more susceptible to excessive effects.

Her eyelashes fluttered as it wrapped her, and she slumped as the pain tightening her features eased.

Cade pulled away quickly, not wanting her to pass out. "Lya?"

She stirred, head bobbing. "You know, I was just trying to decide if I'd let you bite me when those assholes showed up."

Her words slurred a little, but she'd stay conscious.

A thrill shot through him, quickly suppressed. "We can talk about that when you're not glamoured and poisoned. Come on, let's get you all the way down."

He eased her flat as carefully as he could, unable to help himself from brushing a curl of hair from her eyes before turning his attention back to her thigh. With her muscles slack and no reaction to the pain other than a groan that sounded much more like pleasure, getting the bullet out was easy.

Cade dropped it on the floor. "What now?"

"Lead bother you?"

"Not at all."

"Then be my guest."

He frowned before realizing what she meant. "You want me to use saliva to close it up?"

"Faster than stitches. Feels better too." She smiled sloppily. "If you want, I mean."

Cade did want. He really, really did. Just the smallest taste to give him something to dream about. *Don't drink. Don't drink. Just stop the bleeding.*

She'd already lost enough that he was debating the wisdom of continuing their hunt. Still, his conviction wavered as he leaned over her thigh, closed his mouth over the wound, and pressed his tongue against it.

Saliva burst forth and blended with magic to kickstart the healing process, even as the taste of her exploded through him. *Don't. Drink. Do not.*

With an effort, he arrested the reflex to bite, limiting himself to cleaning and closing the wound as much as he could. The elf-blooded never quite healed completely, as humans did, but she was right. This was much more effective—and more enjoyable for both of them—than trying to stitch her would be.

"Fuck," he breathed when he pulled away. He needed more.

He needed *her*, all of her, all to himself.

Lya blinked her eyes open and smiled lazily, looking like someone coming down from a high. "Now the other one."

With all the fresh blood, he'd missed the other wound, partly hidden by her shirt. He didn't hesitate this time, burying his face against the front of her flank as he held on to reason by his fingernails.

He almost lost himself closing the exit wound. Three almost-feedings, enough to taste, not enough to have.

If he couldn't have her someday very soon, he was going to go mad.

Cade pushed himself away, squeezing his eyes shut and panting as he dropped his head between his knees. Now it was him trembling, not from poison but from pure need. He'd had the sense to feed this morning, after talking to Torsten's people but before seeking Morris's daylight location in the relative safety of dawn.

It wasn't enough. He'd underestimated the pull of her blood.

"Hey. You okay?" Her hand squeezed his shoulder weakly, and he jumped.

She didn't flinch away from the intensity he knew he was fixing her with when his gaze met hers. Didn't avert her eyes. Maybe because they were still a little unfocused.

There were a dozen things he wanted to say, chief among them asking if she herself was feeling better, but what leaped from his tongue was, "I hope you weren't teasing me about biting you."

He flushed immediately, embarrassed by his lack of couth, but she just smiled lopsidedly.

"I'll cancel the arrangement with Maria when the hunt is done."

His attention sharpened until all he could see was the jump of the pulse in her throat. "You'd do that?"

"Yeah. You could have finished what the elves started just now. You didn't."

"You trusted me. I wouldn't betray that."

Lya looked away, guilt flickering across her face. "Yeah. I guess not."

That snapped him out of his blood lust like a slap to the face. He hadn't meant it as a dig at her for coming after him when he'd trusted her with the location of his nest. "I didn't mean it like that."

"Thanks."

They sat in awkward silence, until she grimaced and hunched again. "Glamour's worn off."

"What do you need now?" A task. He needed a task. Anything to keep him busy and not thinking about the taste still lingering on his tongue.

"Vitamin C to clear the rest of the lead. Needs water." She handed him a box of little packets.

Snatching one, he hurried to the kitchen and dumped the half-finished glass of juice in the sink rather than waste time looking for a fresh glass, refilling it with water and emptying the full packet in. It stank as it fizzed, but she drank it down, grimacing when she was done.

"Thank you," she said. "For all of this. I should be good to go by tomorrow afternoon. Does that still work?"

"Yes. Much better than tonight." He smiled to take the sting out of what he had to say next. "Unlike me, Morris is likely much weaker during the day. But Lya, I have to warn you. I didn't try to take him myself because I'm still his fledgling. He could cloud my mind. Turn me against you. I'm—I might not be the most reliable ally."

She snorted then pushed to her feet and swayed, favoring her left leg before catching herself on the counter. "Then that'd definitely make us even, wouldn't it?" When he couldn't find a response, she said, "I'm going to wash up. Make yourself at home."

Cade took her at her word, ghosting through the house as she showered. When he'd established the main entries and exits and dragged a chair under the front doorknob, he found the second bullet then dug around for cleaner and set about getting the blood out of the carpet—as much to help and to prevent a breaking of the Détente as to reduce the scent load before it really did drive him out of his mind.

Unfortunately, the mindless work left his brain free to fantasize, an endless loop of her moaning with pleasure under him as her blood filled his mouth while he came. He'd made peace with what he'd become after his first death a long time ago, but it'd never tortured him as much as it did now.

He could take her to the heights of pleasure even as he stole her life. Make her enjoy the process in more ways than one.

For the first time in his long life, that horrified him because he realized, in her, he'd found a life partner. Vampires didn't pick mates at all, let alone for life. Some of the more traditional moroi said there was no point when they didn't reproduce sexually.

Cade disagreed. Either way, they did have other connections and relationships, other commitments they could and did make for companionship and other needs, and he couldn't get the idea out of his head once it slipped in.

What would it be like to have a true companion? Someone he didn't have to fear? It wasn't her job to heal the damage done by Morris. But what if he could finally bring himself to love someone?

The water shut off. Light footfalls on the bathroom tile were followed by the soft tearing noise of paper, suggesting she was putting bandages over the not quite closed wounds. Cade wrapped up what he was cleaning and had just about gotten everything put away when Lya emerged, wrapped in a towel and holding a damp cloth. She still looked a little weak and shaky, a little paler than usual, but not like she was on the verge of passing out anymore.

"Better?" Cade asked.

Her brows went up as she took in his work. "A bit, yeah. Thanks for"—she waved her hand at the carpet—"all that. How do you feel about planning horizontally?"

He coughed.

"I mean really planning." Her smile was gentler this time, almost shy. "I could use a lie-down."

"Sure. Okay. Fluids?"

"Please. Um. Juice in the fridge. Glasses in the cupboard next to it. Bedroom's this way." She tilted her head then shuffled in that direction.

She'd changed to some tiny boxer shorts and a thin-strapped top when he followed her. The cloth was over her eyes.

Cade made himself keep moving rather than pause to ogle her. "Your juice, my lady."

With a snort, she lifted the cloth enough to peek at him. "You almost sound like you mean that."

165

"I do."

She pulled the cloth all the way off and pushed herself up against the headboard, suddenly looking much more serious. "I didn't know vamps made attachments like that."

"Most of the time, we don't. There are very few exceptions." He shrugged and set the juice on the bedside table. "I can't explain it. You're just special."

All expression washed from her face so quickly he wondered if he'd mis-stepped.

"You met me a few days ago. How can you know that?"

"I just do." He tilted his head and studied her, reading self-doubt more than anything else.

"Fine." Her brow wrinkled in a frown. Then her features eased as she gestured at the bed, more familiar territory for them than...whatever this was becoming. "Come here."

"My clothes are bloody."

She smirked. "Then take them off."

Cade grinned. "As my lady commands."

He toed off his shoes and stripped down to his briefs, took the hand she extended, and let her pull him closer. Then he carefully climbed over her to the open side of the bed. When he was stretched out beside her on the duvet cover, he propped his head on his hand and studied her, wondering how she'd react if he asked who'd attacked her.

"My boss took exception to some things I said." Lya glanced at him then away. "That's what you're trying to decide if you can ask, right?"

"Yes. I don't like this. But I also won't presume to try to fix it for you."

Her full lips quirked in a small, satisfied smile. "I knew I liked you for a reason."

He held his peace while she drank some of her juice, waiting to see what she was willing to share.

"I can't stay in town, Cade. If Farand doesn't push me into breaking the terms of my exile, then he'll arrange another incident like today. Then another and another, until either I leave or I'm dead."

He scowled. "You have no recourse?"

Her incredulous look said it all. "The system is working as designed. It's not set up to help me. It's set up to benefit the high-bloods. Nobody in the office spoke up today, and none of them will. They're too comfortable where they are, and that comfort is worth more than my life." She shrugged, as though that was that. "So. Cards on the table. I need this hunt for more than just settling things between us. I need to prove I'm useful to Callista or get enough money to run."

At the pleading look in her eyes, he leaned in and kissed her on the forehead. "We'll get it done. For now—"

"For now, tell me what you found out. Please." She shifted onto her uninjured side, bringing her warmth even closer then closer still as she ran a finger down his flank.

Cade leaned in before he caught himself, but she closed the gap and pressed her lips to his. He'd tell her, but first...

First, he needed to reassure himself she was still here. Still alive.

She might shrug off what had happened as her lot in life, but he'd be damned if he would—and he needed her to know that someone cared about her. Because as their kiss deepened, he realized he wasn't sure what he'd do if anything like this happened to her again.

What he did know was that the other party wouldn't survive.

Chapter 19: Lya

I woke just before dawn the next day, my natural crepuscular rhythm at work despite having been up most of the night alternating between making out with Cade and making plans to hunt Morris. My vampire—and I flushed at thinking of him that way, although I undeniably did—was stretched out on his stomach beside me, naked as Adam under the sheets, given that we'd had to wash my blood out of his clothes. His pupils had stayed dilated, probably at the lingering scent of blood even I could smell, but he kept his fangs behind his lips. He'd crashed a few hours ago, his usual nocturnalism overridden by having been up all of the previous night and most of the next day. Being pushed into overload dealing with me didn't help.

I suspected he thought he'd hidden his thoughts fairly well, but I could read people. Farand's name was filed in the back of his mind. He wouldn't try to fix anything for me now, but if Farand tried attacking me again, there'd be hell to pay. I couldn't find it in myself to feel bad about that or to warn Cade off.

Fuck, I *liked* it. It gave me the warm and fuzzies like nobody's business, to have someone care that much.

Was it dysfunctional? Probably. Was I bothered? Not at all.

Especially not when it was combined with the care he took with how deeply he glamoured me and not so much as a graze of his fangs as he healed me.

That had been something else. It was different when there was a sexual component and not just an arranged bite, like I had with Maria. I couldn't help the way my mind wandered to how that'd feel in bed, the high of glamour blended with erotic gratification and then that little lance of pain transmuted into new pleasure…

As though he could scent my body's response to that thought, Cade stirred, taking one of the deep inhales vampires seemed to need every so often, undead or not. I reached out to comb his hair back from his face, and he came awake and caught my wrist so quickly that I gasped.

"Sorry," he muttered, releasing me as he placed himself. Then he smirked. "Usually you're trying to run away in the morning, not be sweet."

I tried to scowl, but he was right. And he was cute when he was sleepy. I settled for sticking my tongue out at him.

"How're your wounds?" He hugged the pillow, the picture of innocence and good behavior.

"Good question." I peeled the bandage away from the front of my abdomen to reveal a tender, mostly healed scab. After finding my thigh almost as good, I rolled to my stomach to let him get the bandage over the exit wound on my back.

He kissed it then ran a lazy finger down my spine. "Almost good as new. You had me worried yesterday. I didn't realize you'd heal that fast."

"I didn't used to. Maria said I was starting to heal faster."

Cade grunted then kissed my back again before flopping onto his own. "Repeated exposure to vampire saliva with some human blood in your heritage can do that. It won't save you from another event like yesterday, but yes, you'll recover faster." His voice dropped to an angry growl. "Assuming you survive, that is."

I snuggled closer, startled for a moment when I rested my head on his chest and didn't hear a heartbeat. Then it gave a slow, heavy thump before going quiet again. That was going to take some getting used to, as was the unusually cool dryness of his skin.

But I could deal with it. I was starting to think there was a lot I could deal with if it meant keeping Cade around.

His arm came around me to hold me closer, and we both dozed off again, needing a little more rest before kicking off our hunt. Kind of like lions, seeming lazy until we had somewhere to be. It wasn't like I had to go to work anymore. I wasn't about to show up at the bail bond agency today or any other day.

Yeah, it was part of the terms I'd agreed to that I'd make myself useful, but Farand had explicitly said to get the hell out and not come back.

Was that a trap? Probably.

But I felt safe curled up against Cade, in a way I hadn't in ages.

I carried that feeling with me when we finally dragged ourselves out of bed a couple hours later. Cade fetched the laundry I'd had him throw in with his clothes while I dressed and geared up. He followed suit, tucking my CUB knife behind his belt and hefting the Sawback machete I loaned him before swinging it in a few quick movements like it was a sword.

Of course. He'd been a pirate.

Then he watched with a worried frown as I stretched and twisted, limbering the stiff muscles in my flank and thigh. They were healed—mostly—but I wasn't a hundred percent quite yet. Still, I could walk, and that meant I could hunt. I didn't have a choice.

"I'll be fine," I said.

He just nodded, still looking concerned as he sheathed the Sawback and easily shouldered the bag of weapons I'd thrown together last night. He also grabbed the cooler I'd pulled out when he mentioned picking up blood from his place as a safety measure—I might be willing to let him bite me, but in a fight wasn't the best time.

I went up on tiptoes to kiss him. "Thanks for saving my ass yesterday and for letting me do this."

"I don't think I could let or not let you do anything." He smiled wryly then stole another kiss. "Shall we?"

Cade opened the door, inhaling deeply then shaking his head when he didn't find any elven scent. I led the way to my car and hopped in the driver's seat while he put the kit in the back.

"I still think I should go in first," he said as he slid into the passenger seat.

"That'd just mean I'll have two vampires to deal with if he manages to twist your mind." I offered a wry smile as I got the car going and on our way. "That didn't work out so well for me last time, and I have a funny feeling Morris could do something about your self-control. If you find him first, leave him to me."

He grimaced and something haunted entered his eyes. "Fair."

I didn't love that item on the list of potential disasters, but Cade had reasoned that if Morris could have taken him the other night rather than just addle him, he would have; ergo, he couldn't. I didn't know enough to say otherwise.

We spent the drive to Raleigh fine-tuning our plan, but Cade stiffened as soon as we reached his door, although nothing looked off to me.

My hand drifted to my purse, where I had my Walther PPK loaded for vamp or were. "What?"

"Another of us has been here," he murmured, nostrils flaring as his grip tightened on the cooler. He tested the doorknob, and it swung open to reveal a shambles. "Shit. Wait here."

Before I could object, he dropped the cooler and moved inside a little too quickly for human. I glanced up and down the corridor with a wince, relieved we were the only ones around. He was back a few seconds later.

"It's clear. But it's a mess." Fury tinged both his words and his expression, and I waited for him to back up a bit before following him inside. There wasn't a stick of furniture left undamaged, and the fancy fridge holding the spare blood—what we'd come here for—was in the middle of the living room floor. "Not strong enough to rip a padlock off yet, fortunately."

"What do you mean? You know who was here?"

Cade frowned, deep in thought. "No. But my guess is that Morris has stolen a fledgling. He can't have made another of his own. He's too weak still. But he could cloud a younger one's mind and pull them away from a weaker master."

"You can do that?"

"I can't. But a city-level master like Torsten could for a few hours, and Morris was at least that strong before I burned him. It's poor form, but he's clearly desperate enough to try it." He gave me a grim look.

"Don't even say it. I'm not staying behind." I dropped the cooler and sent it his way with a foot. Not like the wood floors could get any more scratched than they already were.

"Fine. Then let's get this done before we lose the daylight." He fished his keys from his pocket, opened the fridge, and scooped the few packets into the cooler.

One, he started to tuck behind his waistband, and I held out a hand. "You want it warmer?"

With a lopsided smile, he pitched it my way, and I tucked it under my shirt, where my body heat would warm it. He'd need this one for a little boost before the fight and the other two for after if he got hurt.

"You can't come back here," I blurted as I looked around the space. Whatever he'd built here was gone. "It might not be this fledgling next time, and either way, it's unlivable."

He looked up sharply. "I know that."

I chewed my lip then made a decision that felt fast but right. "So, get your shit. We'll take it with us, and then whatever happens after, we're both ready."

Gratitude broke through the scowl. "Thank you."

After a last sweep to salvage what clothes hadn't been completely shredded and a handful of personal effects that'd survived, he put his cap and sunglasses back on and led the way back down to my car, a big suitcase in one hand and the cooler in the other. His jaw was set with anger as he stowed it in the back, and I didn't bother trying to make small talk.

I took us around the corner and parked in the public lot on New Bern and South East, ignoring the sign insisting on monthly accounts only. We couldn't risk looking suspicious to the neighborhood's residents or being spotted by Morris on the off chance he was up. From what Cade had said, the neighbors might not notice much of anything anyway, but eventually someone would ask questions about pattern deviations and look for traffic cam footage. I didn't need my SUV coming up on any bulletins.

After Cade downed the blood like it was one of those fruity juice drink pouches we slipped out, caps and sunglasses on, heads down, and wearing the high-vis vests from my emergency car kit in the hopes we'd be taken for construction workers. There was a lot of work going on downtown, and nobody paid much attention to workers unless they were catcalling.

Cade walked slightly ahead, leading the way to the house he'd tracked Morris to, exuding enough glamour that the few humans on the street didn't notice us, let alone the badly concealed weapons we carried.

I frowned as we walked up the short driveway like we had a reason to be there. The street was strangely quiet other than the habitual busyness of the city. The grass was slightly overgrown, and abandoned toys lay in the yard of the house next door. Might just mean the kids were at school. Might be a little more sinister. I hoped not. Kids made cover-ups complicated. I said a silent prayer they were at school and unaware of what was going on in the neighborhood.

With a last look exchanged between us, I knocked on the door. A risk but if there were still mundanes here, we had to get them out first. Othersiders might feed on humans, turn them, or kill them, but it had to be only when strictly necessary and only as a last resort or it'd be in violation of the Détente that kept us all off their radar.

A man answered the door. He looked far paler than even his natural skin tone would account for, and he smelled unwashed. Stringy blond hair fell untidily over his forehead.

The glaze of his eyes suggested a glamour.

"Can I help you?" he asked through the screen door.

I injected more of a Southern twang into my accent. "Hello, sir. Looking for a man named Morris about a property question. That you?"

The man's eyes widened, and even I could smell his fear. Cade grunted but said nothing.

"Sir?" I drew on Aether and put a little push behind it, glad I had enough magic to make mundanes more amenable to answering questions. "Is Morris available?"

"You need to leave." Fear broke through the glamour, making him pant, and he glanced back into the depths of the house. "Please. He'll kill my family. He told me if anyone—"

"Easy, sir. Be easy." I pushed a little more Aether before his agitation could trigger someone else in the house then lowered my voice and took a risk. The Détente had already been broken. At this point, I was actually helping, for once. "We know what he is. We can help, but you need to get anyone not like him out of the house. You understand?"

Wild hope sprang into his eyes before something inside him crushed it. "I have to tell him you've come for him. He said—"

"No! No, stay here. Are you able to open the door?"

"No. Nobody can come in or out."

"Can you resist the instructions for a minute?"

He grimaced, straining. "Yes."

"Fine. Don't move." I got out my lockpick kit and made short work of the screen door's lock, swinging it open to let Cade in first.

"Where?" Cade said quietly.

The man clutched his head, and his throat corded as though he was holding in a scream before gasping, "Master bedroom. Closet."

"Easy." I laid a hand on his arm and tried a little more Aether, enough that the mundane's nose wrinkled at the scent of burnt marshmallow only now breaking through to him. "Take me to your family."

While Cade went to investigate the situation with Morris, I followed the homeowner to the kitchen. A dark-skinned woman and two kids—theirs, it looked like—sat at a table. She looked just as drawn as the man did, but fortunately, the kids looked fine other than being scared.

"Do you have somewhere you can go?" I asked.

"My mother's." The woman's eyes were glazed as well, but their depths sparked despite the slowness of her words. "But he won't let us leave."

"My friend and I will take care of that. Write down your phone numbers and the address for your mother for me, okay? When it's safe to come home, I'll let you know."

I felt a little sick at the lie.

It wasn't to let them know when they could come home. It was so that Callista or Torsten could send in a damage control

175

team. The Darkwatch would have to make them forget this. We couldn't be Revealed to human society. Certainly not like this.

I had to give her credit though. She pulled herself together and, with a shaking hand, scrawled down what I'd asked for. I pocketed the paper then held out a hand when they jumped at Cade's sudden reappearance in the kitchen.

"He's still there," he growled, wincing when I raised my eyebrows at him for his tone then tilted my head at the assembled humans.

With a sigh, he pulled off his sunglasses. "Look at me."

They obeyed, whether out of desperation or the conditioning of the last few days.

"Go to the address you gave her." He met their eyes in turn as the weight of a glamour flooded the space. "Don't speak of this or us being here. You were having some family troubles and thought a change of pace would help even things out."

"Okay," all the humans said at once. We trailed them to the door and watched them get in their car with nothing but what they were wearing, their wallets, and their keys.

"We need to make this fast," I said. "Somebody is going to ask some tough questions soon."

The curtains in the master bedroom were closed tight, and the closet had been blocked shut by something heavy on the other side. I didn't bother opening the curtains. The sunlight might help us against Morris, but it'd also potentially mean human witnesses to us killing him and then doing whatever we had to do to cover it up.

Cade and I stared at the door. Me, as I mentally reviewed the plan one more time. Him with thoughts of his own, worry pinching the skin around his eyes.

"Lydia," he said.

I looked up at the sharpness in his voice, wondering where he'd gotten my full name.

"Don't let anything happen to yourself."

"Okay?"

Before I could blink, he caught me with a hand, cupping the base of my skull. "Do not. Let anything. Happen."

He kissed me with an urgency I didn't understand but responded to without thought, opening my mouth for his. When he pulled away, I took a breath to recover my thoughts as he caressed my cheek with a thumb.

"You break it down, I go in," I whispered.

Cade nodded and squared up on the closet door, having already tried to open it the usual way. With his first solid kick, the wood around the doorknob splintered, but the door caught on something.

The second sent it flying open as he stumbled back.

Gun up, I darted past him, catching broken wood against my shoulder as it rebounded. The huge walk-in had been blocked on the other side by a stepladder wedged under the door. The end of my silencer pointed at an upright and very awake old-ass vampire—taller than me or Cade, skeletally thin, strings of lanky, white hair, and blue eyes that burned with a blend of rage and hatred for a moment before twisting to glee.

Chapter 20: Lya

I didn't waste time swearing, just fired. I got three shots off before he was on me, carrying me down to the floor with him on top. He darted in for a bite, and I jabbed my left fist into his throat.

With a roar, Cade grabbed Morris and threw him across the bedroom.

The old bastard hit the far wall with a crack that had to be something breaking and not just the picture frames filled with family photos. Cade leaped after him as I scrambled to my feet.

"Move, Cade! I don't have a shot!"

Too late.

Morris looked up—and Cade froze in place. I sidestepped, trying to get clear, but Morris did the same in the opposite direction, keeping Cade between us.

He laughed, a dry cackle that could have been equally due to his decrepit state as the throat punch I'd dealt him. "So. My dear fledgling comes home at long last and brings an apology gift with him. You must be very special, girl. In the centuries I had him, I couldn't tempt him once with a partner. Yet here you are. That was sweet, his little order before breaking my door down." He sniffed Cade's neck and smiled wider. "I can smell you on him. And in him? Have you shared yourself with him? I wonder, what would he do if I drained you?"

Cade's eyes widened, and he jerked. A groan slipped from him.

"Shhh, dear boy. Don't worry. I'll let you watch. I might even let you take her last blood when I grow bored of the screaming."

My stomach clenched. This was a mess. A hot, stinking mess we'd walked right into. I didn't like how much stronger Morris was than we'd planned on.

I had an option: shoot through Cade and hope the bullet passed through Morris as well.

Silver would poison them both, but Cade had a better shot at recovery.

I hoped.

The older vampire smiled as though he'd read the thought. "You see, I only let him *think* I was too weak to take him. I saw you together the other night and thought, why not have them both? Such a pretty pair." He draped himself across Cade's shoulders and caressed his chest with an intimacy that turned my stomach and made me snarl.

Every muscle in Cade's body tensed and his fists clenched, but he didn't do anything to move away. Couldn't, from the way he shook.

"Get away from him." I squeezed the butt of my Beretta, wishing for just one clear shot.

"I think not. Look at me, girl."

I didn't, darting to the side again, only for Morris to jerk Cade around between us.

"I suppose we will do this the hard way then."

Pain flashed across Cade's face as Morris twisted his arm up and behind him, dislocating his shoulder, and sank his teeth into his wrist.

I had no shot at Morris's head that wouldn't take Cade's too.

179

Mind racing, I sought an option. Any other option. But I didn't have time to think, not if Morris was willing to drain Cade so he could take his leisure with me.

I'd be damned if I let that happen.

I raised my gun, not daring the risk of looking into Cade's eyes for permission or forgiveness, but I caught the tight bob of his chin. He'd rather be shot by me than have both of us captured and tortured by Morris.

Fine.

Morris must have caught the movement because he looked up and cocked his head. "You would really shoot him to get to me?"

I didn't answer, just aimed at Cade's belly, where I hoped there'd be a better chance of a through-and-through. My own gut twinged in sympathy.

But before I could fire, Morris said, "Let me save you the anguish."

In a flash of movement, he pulled my silver-edged CUB knife from behind Cade's belt and stabbed his fledgling in the throat.

"No!" I screamed as Cade dropped, already gagging on blood.

"Save him or shoot me?"

I was firing before he finished speaking—and missed as Morris launched himself over the bed at me.

We went down again. The Beretta went spinning from my hand. I scrambled after it, only to be dragged back. Morris cackled, enjoying himself, and made a mistake Cade hadn't when I'd fought him: he didn't stop me from speaking.

In desperation, I drew on as much Aether as I could and lashed out at his mind. "Get. Off. Me!"

It didn't work as well as it would have on a human, but it gave him a blessed heartbeat of pause. Long enough for me to scrabble away. My hand closed on the butt of the gun.

As Morris's hand closed around my ankle again, I twisted and fired.

The bullet took him square between the eyes.

As the master vampire fell back, I pushed away and to my feet, emptying the clip into him. He thrashed on the floor, fighting the pain of silver poisoning, as I rushed to Cade's side. Blood made the carpet sodden under him, and panic rose as I slipped in it. The hand holding the knife in place was loose, and his eyes were distant and unseeing.

Focus. Get the job done.

Snatching the Sawback from where Cade had dropped it, I dashed back to Morris. He swiped at me, fingers hooked to claws, but the silver added to the daylight and the existing weakness from being burned to tip the scales in my favor.

I danced back then lined up and swung the blade hard enough to take his head with one blow. Cade gasped.

I wrenched the machete free and kicked the head far enough away that it couldn't spontaneously reattach. As it bounced into a corner and lodged between the wall and a nightstand, I hurried back to Cade's side. He'd passed out, whether from blood loss or the severing of the tie with his sire, I didn't know. I just knew I had to clean this up and get us out.

I couldn't take Cade back to his nest. That had been compromised—not to mention the fact that a master vampire was dead in Torsten's territory. That Torsten hadn't known about said master didn't matter.

It'd happened, and we were responsible.

I hadn't established any safehouses in my exile, so that left my flat as the sole safe location. Far enough from Raleigh not to piss off the coterie, likewise from Durham not to piss off Callista or the werecats.

Surely nobody would care about Cade when the master who'd put out a bounty on him was twice dead?

181

Except that Torsten might have to make an example, lest his coterie get ideas.

I couldn't risk leaving Cade here.

My place it was.

"Stay here. Stay alive." I didn't wait for Cade to respond before running into the master bathroom to wash the blood off my hands and shoes before chanting a minor "don't see me" spell and tearing out of the house, back down the street to the parking lot.

Wonder of wonders, there was no ticket when I got back to the car.

Every second of the two minutes it took to drive back, reverse into the house's driveway, and block the front window with sun shades passed as an eternity. Cade was exactly where I'd left him, still out cold.

Fortunately, there was enough cover from trees and shrubs that I was able to drag him from a side door of the house and into the back seat of the car.

Maybe twice as lucky, he didn't wake up.

I couldn't leave yet though. I'd been the last Othersider at the scene. If I left before someone else got here for a coverup, it'd be my ass—and I couldn't call Callista and tell her that I'd just killed the bounty client rather than the target.

Maria. Has to be Maria.

This was a vampire issue. If I called her, she could handle it her way. If the Darkwatch got called in, that wouldn't be on me. I fished my phone out and dialed, increasingly aware of the growing scent of old blood and wet ash growing chokingly thick in the car.

As it rang, I dug in the cooler for the last two packs of blood, squeezing them between my thighs. "Come on, come on—Maria!"

"Well hello, doll. Wasn't expecting to hear—"

"Maria, I'm sorry, but it's an emergency. There was a master vampire squatting in a human home on New Bern, next to the cemetery. Glamoured the family and possibly the neighbors to hell and back."

"Excuse me?"

"Look, I'm sitting in the driveway now. The master is dead, Cade's on his way to following, and I can't be here when someone decides to check on the family. Can you handle this?"

"Did you call Callista?" The flirtation and charm had disappeared, leaving cold business and a hint of threat.

"No, I figured she'd call in the Darkwatch and that you wouldn't want elves on your turf."

"Smart cookie. I'll have someone there in ten minutes. Don't leave until they get there."

"Favor for a favor? Cade wasn't here. You found out about this other bloke not following vagabond protocol and used our arrangement to leverage my help." Callista might well have Watchers who would tell her otherwise, but if the Raleigh coterie played ignorant rather than making noise, she'd have no leverage to do anything about it. "We think he stole a fledgling. That should help."

"Hmm. Then I get credit for dealing with a rogue in violation of the Détente and in an act of aggression against the coterie. Fine, that works for me. Do what you can to keep any curious mundanes away."

I didn't bother protesting, just hung up and jabbed the top of the first blood pack with a knife before twisting to hover it over Cade's nose, barely managing not to jostle the knife still in his neck. "Hey. Cade. Come on—"

He caught my wrist and sank fangs into the bag, the knife bobbing with every swallow as he fed mindlessly.

This was not fucking good at all. None of his past control was evident.

When that bag was drained, I wrenched free while he gnawed on the plastic and poked enough of a hole in the second one to tempt him. That one was drained by the time another car pulled up in the street. I freed myself again and opened the car door, standing behind it and holding my gun down at my side.

The other door opened, and I slumped in relief. "Noah."

"Ms. Desmarais." He made his way up the lawn and grimaced as the scents from the car hit him. "Leave him."

"I can't."

"You can, and you should. He's dangerous like this."

"Would Torsten allow the coterie to keep him against Callista's wishes?"

Noah's long stare gave me my answer.

"Then I can't leave him."

"He could kill you. Almost certainly will try."

"Trust me, he's had plenty of chances already."

"But now he has motivation." He shrugged, his irritated expression smoothing. "If you want to play devil's advocate, be my guest. Just know that, if he's as far gone as I think, this devil will claim blood whether you give it willingly or not. None of us will step in one way or the other, but if I don't hear from you in three days, we'll send a cleanup crew to your home for whatever's left."

I nodded, shaky and cold at the idea that he really expected me to die saving Cade's life and didn't care.

Noah waved. "You can leave now. We have this."

"Thank you." I scrambled back into the car, pulled down the shades, and got my ass on the road.

Cade didn't stir the whole way, and I grew increasingly anxious as he didn't respond to anything I said. I forced myself to drive at five over—fast enough to feel like I was getting somewhere, not so fast I'd get pulled over and then have to explain an undead man bleeding to his second death with a knife in his neck and a car full of unregistered weapons.

I gave myself a second to breathe a sigh of relief when I pulled up in front of my flat then realized I had a problem: getting him inside. I didn't have the level of Aether needed to turn attention away from me when that attention was drawn by something as dramatic as a bleeding, unconscious man.

The short distance from my parking spot to my front door had never seemed so long as I sat studying it. The engine pinged as it cooled.

Cade didn't make a single damn noise at all.

"Hey. Cade."

Nothing.

"Cade!"

He groaned.

Okay. Still alive. Or undead, rather. "I have to get you inside, okay?"

Again, no reaction. Shit.

Too many of my neighbors had dogs for me to risk walking a literal corpse in my front door. I was going to have to feed him.

For once, the walkway crossing in front of my apartment was clear. I put the sun shades back in the front windows then clambered into the backseat of the truck, scrunching myself into the footwell next to Cade's head.

The sharp, ash-metal scent of vampire blood filled my car, layered with the acrid scent of silver from the blade's edge. He was going to need a big donation.

Shit.

I was out of options if I wanted him to live, and I did, even if it was going to cost me big.

Fuck it. This was going to hurt, but so be it.

"Cade." I patted his cheek. His eyelids flickered. "Cade, wake the fuck up. Right now."

He must have caught the scent of me because he roused. "Lya?"

"I'm going to get the knife out and give you some blood, okay? But you need to drink fast so I can get you into my flat."

"Blood."

"Yes, dammit. Can you take some and lean on me to get inside?"

No response.

I hesitated, but I was out of options. Working fast, I yanked the knife out and pressed one of the high-vis vests against it before wiping the knife on his shirt.

Then I pressed it to my left wrist. Bit my lip as I steeled myself.

Pressed and dragged, praying I wouldn't have to put it in his heart if he lost control.

The scent of blood blossomed in the tight confines of the car, and Cade perked up immediately.

I pressed my wrist to his mouth before he could do much else and grunted when he gripped my arm and hand so hard bones ground together. The pain of the knife slice was joined by the twin punctures of teeth as he latched on.

A low groan slipped from him as he pulled.

Being a snack without glamour hurt like hell. I swallowed a pained noise, not wanting to push him further over the edge, and shifted so I could lay my head on his chest. His heart went from silent to thudding like he'd run a race, pumping my blood through his system to the most damaged areas.

When he'd had a few swallows, I said, "Okay. Enough."

He gripped tighter, pulled harder.

"Cade. Let go." I put a push of Aether behind it.

With a deep inhale, he released me. I pulled my arm away, clutching it to my chest with alacrity. I studied him. Scented him.

Peeked behind the vest, and was relieved to find the wound oozing only a slow trickle. He was still weak but better.

"Can you walk?" I asked.

"With help."

"Okay." I wrapped my wrist in a bandana. "I'm going to get out and come around to the door nearest your head. I'll help you to my front door, inside, and to my bed where you can rest safely. Then you can drink from me again. Deal?"

His eyelids flickered. "You'll feed me again?"

"Yes. Just…don't kill me." I flushed with shame at the request.

"I won't. I promise. Please…please don't let me die. Please, Lya. Not now."

How the hell could I ignore that?

"Okay. Hang on." I checked out the tinted window. Nobody. Thank fuck. After I slipped out, I muttered my don't-see-me spell again and maneuvered Cade to sit upright. "Ready?"

"Yeah."

He wasn't, based on the flinch when I slung his arm over my shoulder and pulled, but he was trying. It had to be close enough.

"Up we go," I said.

We nearly went down as he slid-stumbled out of the car. I bumped us against the door to shut it then managed his weight to my front door, forcing a giggle and hoping any neighbors who saw this would think he was just a sloppy drunk or something.

"Steady," I murmured as I held him propped up between me and the wall and fished my keys out while looking for danger.

Nothing and no one attacked us as I unlocked my door and staggered in with him then kicked it shut behind me in a jangle of bells. We almost hit the floor again as I took a moment to lock the door behind us then shoved the chair back in front of it and step-tripped to my bedroom.

He groaned as I dropped him on the bed. I knelt on the floor alongside, panting at the effort of carrying practical deadweight significantly heavier than me.

"I'll be back in a minute." Back in the kitchen, I mixed two liters of oral rehydration solution, and snagged a box of cookies, two packs of jerky, and a mesh bag of oranges, knowing I'd need all of it after feeding Cade enough blood to see him to nightfall, when he might rejuvenate some more. My heart pounded at the idea that I was going to trust him to drink from me without killing me.

Maybe I didn't really care if he did. I didn't know. All I knew was I had to try to keep both of us breathing until moonrise.

After ferrying my supplies to the nightstand on the empty side of the bed and drinking a full glass of ORS, I shut the blinds and curtains as tightly as I could and stripped down to my panties and T-shirt.

Cade was unresponsive and cold as I climbed onto the bed next to him.

"Cade." Nothing. I straddled and shook him then thumped his shoulders when he didn't react. "Cade! Wake up!"

He grimaced.

I slapped him, and the grimace turned into a sharp-fanged snarl. I slapped him again. "Wake up!"

When he still didn't move, I slapped him a third time.

That did it.

Before I could think about what was happening, our positions were flipped. I was on my back. Cade was on top, gripping my throat, all humanity gone and eyes fully black as he considered the situation from an all-vampire perspective.

He was in a weird liminal space where he'd had enough blood to hunt for more but was too drained and hungry to be fully rational.

I gasped for breath but didn't fight him.

I'd done this. I'd insisted on going after Morris rather than leaving town, and I hadn't been fast enough to get a good shot in when we busted into the closet. I'd fix it.

"I know you." Cade's voice was empty of everything.

"Yeah," I rasped. I squeezed his wrist. Couldn't help it, even as I resisted a reflexive effort to dislodge it or struggle. That'd just make things worse.

"You give yourself to me?"

I wrestled with a response. He'd completely given himself over to me before, had been prepared to let me capture him to fulfill a bounty that would've been my get-out-of-jail-free card. Otherside law was eye for an eye and blood for blood.

There was only one answer that was fair. "Yes."

His grip tightened. "Look at me."

I worked myself up to it. Met his gaze. Glamour washed through me, and I fell.

The sharp piercing of his teeth in my neck barely registered beyond a stab of ecstasy that shot straight to my groin. I moaned and floated in a deeper glamour than Maria had ever used, thoroughly enjoying the sensation of Cade killing me drop by bloody drop.

The pull of his lips against my neck, the growing warmth of his body against mine. His weight pressing down with greater strength. All of it was pleasure.

Darkness hovered. Flickered.

I sighed. Relaxed into it, sinking deeper. This was okay. It felt good, better than good. Borderline orgasmic. And there was no more Farand. No more Callista. No more Lyon Conclave or House Monteague. No more bullshit or worries or exile. Just pleasure and bliss.

The pull stopped.

"Lya?"

189

I couldn't respond, too lost in glamour and blood loss. Spiraling. Floating.

"No! No no no. Lya!"

My pulse and breath were both coming too fast and too shallow. Much faster than they ever had when I'd let Maria drink from me.

"Lya!"

I slipped away into darkness.

Chapter 21: Cade

The blood coating Cade's tongue and throat was too rich to be human and too sweet to be that of another *moroi*. Sweet and faintly herbal. A hint of rosemary and sage. A zing of power that rejuvenated him far more than usual.

That was enough to give him pause, even in the depths of a thirst driven by near-death.

What stopped his mindless drinking was the distant thought that only one being might care enough to offer him this in his current state because he sure as hell wouldn't have been able to hunt it on his own.

Lya.

He snapped back to a conscious mind and pulled away in alarm.

She lay under him, eyes closed and lips curved in a smile even as her heart and lungs heaved in an effort to keep her alive. She'd fought with him, put down Morris when he'd been completely under his sire's spell, and he'd taken too much. She was dying and didn't even know it, lost in the glamour she'd only let him use once before. Her lack of response when he called her name confirmed it.

"No! No no no. Lya!"

He couldn't give her much back. Not only did he need the blood to stay alive himself, but given how much he'd taken, she might turn if he gave too much back. That was strictly forbidden for several good reasons, most of which had good odds of turning out badly for her. Otherwise, he would have risked it anyway.

Cade leaned in again to heal the bite as much as he could— halfway at best, given her elven heritage, but at least it stopped bleeding—then shook her. "Lya!"

Her eyelids fluttered, and then she slipped deeper into the dangerous level of unconsciousness that said he'd taken too much while she was too deeply glamoured.

No. He couldn't be responsible for killing her. Not her.

But he was low on options. His emergency stash was gone. He vaguely remembered desperately downing the last two bags in the back seat of her car.

His gaze darted around this space as he took in the scent. Her nest. No blood and no one else living here, since she was one of the elf-blooded in exile. Just her. And him, a predator suited perfectly to draining her as dead as he was and not at all to saving her life.

No options.

He had to risk feeding her, at least enough for her to take sustenance.

Cade shifted her up against the pillows and focused on the tenuous link created between them by the glamour he'd laid on her.

"Wake up, Lya." No response. He leaned harder. "Lydia!"

She groaned. When her eyelids fluttered enough for him to catch her gaze, he snared her in another glamour. It was dangerous, but he had no choice. "Listen to me."

"Cade?"

"Yes. I need you to drink from me. Just a little."

She blinked. Blinked again. Frowned. "Can't."

"You have to, love, or you'll die. I'm sorry. I didn't mean to take so much."

A shudder ran through her, and she grimaced. "Hurts."

That wasn't good. That wasn't good at all. The glamour should have spared her all pain. If she was feeling it, she was on the edge. Sure enough, her already fast pulse quickened under his hand.

"Lya, you didn't owe me this. Blood for blood, it wasn't—"

She smiled. "I did."

"I say you didn't. Let me feed you. Please. Just a little."

She winced again. Panted.

Risks be damned. He couldn't let her die. "Come on, Lya. I won't give you enough to turn you. I promise. Please."

"Okay."

Cade bit deeply into his own wrist and pressed it to her mouth, massaging her throat when she didn't swallow the first spurt on her own. She groaned when she did and clasped his arm with the urgent need of a fledgling.

He let her take one more swallow then gently pulled away.

Propping her against him, he reached for the glass she'd left on the nightstand next to a bag of jerky, a plate of cookies, and a bag of oranges, and held it to her lips. "This one now, love."

She turned her head aside. Like a fledgling would. Had he given her too much of his blood? Even those small sips?

"Come on, Lya. Please. You need to replenish your fluids."

After enough heartbeats to scare him, Lya latched onto the glass and drank deep.

Cade wrestled with the urge to collapse in relief and steadied the glass, tipping it more as she swallowed more, managing to get more of it down her throat than spilled on her chest. When it was half gone, he pulled it away and held a cookie in front of her nose.

No response.

He swapped it for a piece of jerky, hoping her elven side would kick in and the predator in her would waken.

193

She snapped at that, nearly taking the tips of his fingers with it.

Cade didn't care. He just prayed to Hekate as he cradled her against him, feeding her jerky a piece at a time with sips of whatever strange water was in the glass in between. By the time water and jerky were both gone, she was steadier. He got up and refilled the cup with tap water, offering her that and the cookies. She took both, slower than she had before, until all that was gone as well.

At the last cookie, she turned her head aside. He dropped it onto the plate and shifted back against the bed's headboard before drawing her up against his chest and wrapping his arms around her. She might hate him when the sun came up, but he'd do what he could to keep her warm and comfortable until then.

It was the least he owed her after nearly killing her.

***

Dawn startled him in a way he hadn't experienced in years. No blackout curtains here. He eyed the angle of the sun and relaxed when he determined it wouldn't hit the bed. Waking up here yesterday had been similar, the unfamiliar light and the warmth of—

Lya.

She slept on, still curled against him. Her color was better, and her pulse was stronger. She was warmer too, almost back to being the spot of sunshine he'd quickly come to love waking up next to. She'd need a lot more protein and fluids, and she'd probably have a hellacious headache when she woke up.

But she'd live.

She might hate him, especially if there were ill effects from the two swallows of blood he'd pressed on her, but at least she'd be alive for it. He hoped.

He should go figure out if she had enough to eat, but he couldn't bring himself to leave her. Protectiveness filled him as surely as her blood had, and he hoped that was just a factor of how much he'd taken, not that he'd turned her.

Anxiety crested, enough that his heart started beating. Had he turned her?

I didn't. I couldn't have turned her. It takes much more than two swallows.

But the only time a *moroi* drank as deeply as he had was with intent to kill. Or from a trusted pet.

Ah. Physiological response to a prime source of blood.

He'd never taken a blood pet before and didn't intend Lya to be one, but he'd fed well and the donor was still living, which triggered a set of responses. Just to be sure it really was simple protectiveness of a blood source and not something deeper, he inhaled deeply. She carried some of his scent, but not enough to be his fledgling. He'd never made one, but he'd reeked of Morris's scent for centuries, even after his sire's near-death. He knew what would happen, and it hadn't happened here.

Somewhat reassured, he moved on to debating whether it'd be better for him to be here or gone when she woke up.

The decision was made for him as she gasped in a breath. Her eyelids fluttered before she squeezed them shut and curled tighter into a fetal position. A hard shudder wracked her.

"Cade?" she croaked.

"I'm here."

"Am I dead?"

He almost laughed then realized it might well be a serious question rather than an expression of the shittiness of dehydration. "No. It might feel like it, but no."

"You're still here."

"It seemed the gentlemanly thing to make sure you woke up."
The thought struck him that maybe she'd meant she wanted him
gone. "I could go if you wished."

"No," she said quickly. After another quick grimace of pain,
she added, "Please stay?"

That warmed him even more than her blood had. She *wanted*
him here? She trusted him not to finish the job?

"Okay. Of course." He started to settle against her again then
paused. "Can I get you something?"

"I wouldn't say no to a peeled orange and the other pack of
jerky in the kitchen pantry. And an ibuprofen or four."

With a quick kiss to her temple, Cade slipped out of bed and
made his way to the kitchen. The ray of sun coming in the patio
window didn't bother him nearly as much as it should have, but
he closed all the blinds and curtains anyway. If it hadn't been for
Lya's gift, he'd still be much closer to his second death, unable
to do much more than feed mindlessly. Certainly not be up and
about fetching food and medicine.

Small blessings.

He winced at considering Lya's near-death as a blessing, but
for him, it had been. He'd honor it and move on. She hadn't
asked for it, but he found more juice in the fridge and grabbed
that as well.

She was still curled up in a ball of misery when he brought it
all back to the bedroom.

Cade mentally cursed himself for his lack of control. It hadn't
been completely gone, or she'd be dead. If he didn't love her as
much as he did she certainly would be dead now.

That thought caught him by surprise. Love her. Deeply.
Unquestioningly.

Yes, he cared about her, but real love was a new idea, even if
the word had been tripping off his tongue for days. It swirled in

his brain as he made space for the new provisions, cleared away what she'd finished last night, and then rejoined her in bed.

"I'm sorry, Lya." The words jumped from him before he could find something more eloquent. "I truly am."

"Don't be," she croaked. Grimacing, she drank some of the juice, and he couldn't help but watch her bite-marked throat as she did. "Let's call it even now, hey? Otherwise, we'll go round and round again trying to figure out who's at fault or who owes the other. I just want to…exist. With you." Her cheeks, paled by blood loss, flushed faintly.

"Deal." He edged closer and extended an arm. As he'd hoped she would, she leaned into him and let him pull her closer. For once, he was the warmer of the two of them.

"Callista will have heard about Morris by now," she said after a few more mechanical bites of jerky. "My bet is she calls in the next hour. Probably with threats. The question is whether she has any proof it was me who killed Morris. My gun's unregistered, and I haven't used that particular one on a bounty before. So even if she brings the Darkwatch in, there'll be no record of the bullets to compare to. And that assumes Noah missed one on cleanup."

"You had Noah do cleanup?"

"Maria. I traded a favor, and she sent him."

"Lya—"

"Don't worry. We're not in her debt."

"We?"

Lya squirmed a little under his arm. "I told her that, in exchange for calling her rather than Callista, I wanted no mention of you being there."

Cade stared at the top of her head, trying to figure out what had been going on inside it. "Why?"

"Because if you were there, I can't imply *I* was the one who trashed your place in an effort to fulfill the bounty. If you're"—

she waved her free hand—"anywhere else, then I went after Morris on an anonymous tip passed along by Maria, who wanted to leverage our arrangement and had no idea of the tie between you and him or him and Callista. Maria and I look smart for maintaining the Détente. You have the source of the bounty eliminated. You're free to leave town, and I..." She picked at the blanket. "I don't know what happens to me. I guess Callista will have to arbitrate with Houses Monteague and Desmarais on the terms of my exile."

As she finished the bag of jerky, Cade sat with that. It was clever. Beyond clever.

Lya had taken a shitty situation and turned it to her advantage—and even more, his—quite neatly. He was truly free for the first time since he'd first set sail centuries ago. He'd still have to watch his back, but he'd just survived his worst nightmare. The memory of being in Morris's clutches again would haunt him for a while, but he could leave it behind.

The thought that he wasn't going anywhere without her bubbled to the top of his mind, but he kept it to himself.

His troubles were over. Hers were getting worse. They needed to focus on that for now.

She sighed. "I need more protein. I don't heal elf-fast, but I'll recover faster than a human would if I eat like a werewolf for the next few days."

"Let me make you breakfast then." He couldn't fix her exile situation, but at least he could do that.

Lya slanted a look at him. "You can cook? Beyond boiling a bag of blood?"

"Scrambled eggs aren't difficult."

Her expression said everything, but when she wavered after getting out of bed and had to catch herself on the wall, she relented. "Okay then, Chef Vampire, I'll have a triple serving of bacon and eggs, if you please."

"Coming right up." He headed for the kitchen when she raised an eyebrow like she'd hit him if he tried to help her there. By the time she made it and dropped heavily into a chair, he had the pans heating and the eggs cracked.

As if pouring them into the pan was a cue, her phone rang. She looked at it, took a deep breath, and answered. "Hi Callista."

Cade looked up sharply from scrambling eggs, and Lya put the call on speaker.

"What can I do for you?" Lya said.

"Have you taken Cade yet?"

His blood froze and anxiety spiked.

Lya looked like she was feeling about the same as she paled. "I'm actually recovering from the fallout of my first attempt."

"The client is dead." Callista's low, dangerous tone said she knew something was afoot and was more than willing to do violence to discover it. "Would you happen to know anything about that?"

Lya glanced worriedly at him and swallowed. "Dead? That's a damn shame. I'm out quite a bit on time and supplies. Farand is pissed as well, since I skipped work to try getting this done faster."

Not a lie but not an answer either.

Silence stretched. "Farand had quite a bit to say about you as well, my dear. Why don't you come on up to the bar. We need to have words."

Chapter 22: Lya

I negotiated a day to recover before meeting Callista. Cade offered to find a hotel for that time, and I told him that was bollocks. His flinch of relief suggested he still felt bad about nearly draining me, but I was over it. It'd been my choice. I didn't dwell on past choices. Nobody had died except the asshole who was supposed to, so I moved on.

While I recovered, Cade detailed my car and got anything else I might want to take with me packed and set out next to the door. His stuff was neatly lined up next to mine, as much in limbo as I was. I couldn't take it to the bar in case Callista sent a Watcher out to be nosy, but I also wasn't expecting any real kind of time to get the hell out of town if that was her judgment.

I'd lose the deposit on the flat unless I could buy another favor from Maria but whatever. I'd leave with my life.

Finally, it was time to face the Arbiter. I went alone and drove with the windows open to disperse the smell of Cade on me, seeing as it would kill my story for me to turn up with hints of the vampire I was supposed to have been busy hunting down clinging to me. The June heat was getting worse with every day that crept closer to July, and the humidity made it weigh even heavier as a thunderstorm brewed on the horizon. It echoed my mood as I made my way through downtown, wondering if this was the last time I'd see that bull statue.

The bar was exactly the same as before, even had a few of the same people. I approached the bar, and Callista immediately pointed to her back room. I followed her, stomach churning, and waited for her curt order to sit before taking the cracked leather chair in front of her worn desk.

She stared me down, green eyes sparking like flame-lit emerald. "The only reason I don't kill you for interfering in my business is because I have no proof you knew there was a connection between Cade and Morris, and Maria is saying she wanted Morris removed. You expect me to believe you knew absolutely nothing about Cade before this?"

Did that mean she hadn't had Watchers in Raleigh?

I said nothing. Didn't move a muscle. Just met her glare as solidly as I could.

My silence seemed to piss her off further. "Nothing to say for yourself?"

"No, ma'am."

"Nothing to say for Cade?"

I stared at her, wondering if it would be better or worse if I did.

"Well?"

I gambled and prayed it wouldn't cost Cade his life after everything I'd done to preserve it. "No. Nothing."

Fury sparked in every line of her form and features. "Fine. Get the fuck out of North Carolina. You have two hours before I eliminate the annoyance you represent and send your head to Farand to get him to shut the hell up about disrespect. I may not be able to prove anything about collusion between you and Cade, but I won't have you in my territory making trouble."

Startled, I blurted, "But the terms of my exile— The queens—"

"Don't rule in the Triangle or the Carolinas. I do. I did Houses Monteague and Desmarais a favor letting you settle here.

They owe *me*, not the other way around. And now, my darling one, so do you. Live out your exile anywhere else and count yourself lucky I let you keep that sorry life."

I bit back an exclamation that it wasn't fair. I'd done nothing to merit exile to begin with, but now that I was here, I was exactly as guilty as she thought I was.

I was lucky I could pay the debt with something other than my life.

"I'm so glad we understand each other." Her smile was venom. "If you do know where Cade is, take him with you. Or don't, I don't care. But you're both banished from the Carolinas until I call in my favor. And Lydia? You'd best come running when I do."

"I understand."

She stared at me hard, as though that'd make her point stick, then waved in a sharp dismissal. I wasn't too proud to hustle out, not stopping in my headlong rush until I was home and barreling through my own front door.

"We have to go. Right now," I said as soon as I was in. I didn't even pause before grabbing a suitcase and hauling it back out to the car. I still needed recovery time, but for now, I was fueled by adrenaline and fear. I blew back into the house.

"Stop." Cade caught me when I tried to ignore him. His pupils dilated as my fear hit him, but that was all. His grip tightened just enough to halt me when I tried to break away and eased when I focused on him. "Lya, sit down. What happened?"

"We keep our lives. But we have to get the fuck out of town. Today. Now."

"Do you know where you want to go? Where you'll be safe?"

My stomach plummeted as I shook my head. "I— No. I can't go home, to Europe, even if I wanted to. This is all I have here. It's all I know."

I looked around the flat then at my few belongings clustered by the door. I'd never really settled in. Never even bought a TV or a microwave. It was as though I'd always expected I'd have to leave suddenly or like this was never meant to be a home away from home.

"Are you... Do you want to come with me?"

He smiled. "I'd like to, if you'll have me, and if you will, I have an idea. For now, eat something. I'll load the car. Okay?"

"Okay." My heart skipped, and my stomach fluttered.

I wasn't completely alone. Not completely lost.

While he took care of the bags, I focused on eating what was left in my fridge. Good thing I'd needed to go grocery shopping; I wouldn't be out too much money in food. It all sat in my stomach like lead though, heavy and poisonous, even if it steadied me.

When everything that would fit in or atop the Escape was loaded, I made a last sweep and then headed out to the car.

Cade slid into the passenger seat. "Wait. Breathe, love," he said when I hit the ignition button. "Are you okay?"

"I don't know." I squeezed the steering wheel, closing my eyes to say a quick prayer before getting us on the road. "She can't prove anything. She'll write off the favor she gave the Lyon Conclave, but I owe her one instead."

"You're sure you trust me to come with you?" He spoke so softly I almost asked him to repeat himself.

"Why wouldn't I?"

"I just want you to be sure you'll have me after I nearly drained you. That you're not still protecting me out of guilt for coming after me."

I sat with that a moment while waiting for the traffic light to change. I'd never had a companion like that. Someone who'd just...trust me. Someone I could fuck up with and we could work through it in our own way.

"I'm not," I said. "I'd really like that. Us staying together, I mean."

Cade grinned wide enough to flash fangs and shifted to stay out of a sunbeam as I took the curving onramp to I-40 East. "Good. Because I don't have a car. But I do have some prime beach town property."

"You do?"

"How do you feel about Florida?"

"Never been." It was my turn to smile as some of the dread pooling in my middle drained away. I was a stranger in a strange land, with no idea where to go. If Cade knew and I could get us there, I'd be okay.

We'd be okay. I'd have to drive fast to get us out of North Carolina before the two hours were up, but it was better than the grave. Especially if I had him with me.

***

Cade's little house was tucked away down a short dirt drive off a cobbled side street near downtown St. Augustine, hidden among live oaks draped with long, tangled streamers of Spanish moss. Between the moss, the palmettos, and the overgrown hibiscus bushes, there was an effective privacy screen behind a wooden fence. The distant sounds of live music and tourists enjoying themselves in bars reached us but not loud enough to be annoying. I could smell the salt tang of the distant ocean over the muddy scent of the nearer St. Johns River. Goddess only knew how long this little patch of paradise would be here with the increase in hurricanes, but for now, it was the perfect haven.

I was exhausted after the eight-hour drive, but the big steak dinner I'd gotten on his dime when we'd stopped in town for him to hunt was rejuvenating me. Between that and the fresh, clean air blowing in off the ocean, I was feeling better than I had in months. I set about checking the perimeter and getting a sense for security and defensibility while Cade hurried about inside, opening windows to air the slightly musty scent and putting fresh linens smelling of the cedar chest they'd been stored in on the bed.

If nothing else, at least we had a place to sleep…among other things.

Candles flickered when I made my way back in. Their light danced over Cade's handsome features.

He looked nothing like the arrogant rich guy I'd first met in the Raleigh club. He was more real now. More himself, somehow, in jeans and a black V-neck tee that hugged his muscles. He also looked much more awake now that the sun was down—he'd spent most of the drive passed out in a vampiric stupor, only rousing at sundown to give me directions near the Florida border—and way more relaxed now that we were on turf he knew.

"We safe?" I asked.

He nodded, not taking his eyes off me.

"You have plans for tonight?"

Another nod as something primal slipped behind his gaze. I swallowed, and he stiffened as the scent of my anticipation hit him.

"I hope those plans involve that bed," I said softly. "I mean, I need a shower first but—"

"No. I want you. Now." He eyed me. "If you're up to it."

With a shiver of desire, I took a step toward him. Then another. Slid my arms around his shoulders.

I kissed along his jaw and down his neck. He buried his face in my hair and gripped my hips firmly, pulling me flush against him. The blood he'd drunk earlier worked fast, and he was more than ready.

His fingers tightened as he pulled me backward and led me into the small bedroom. "Do you know how hard it is to be in a car with you all day and *not* touch you?"

"You were asleep!"

"Asleep and dreaming of you."

The growl of his voice sent a line of fire through me, and I thought back to my own scrambled fantasies as our scents blended in my car and adrenaline pushed me to speed south. "I might have been a little distracted while driving myself."

"Then you'll forgive me this."

I gasped as he tugged then spun me, and I fell backward onto the bed. Cade pounced to follow me, pinning my body under his.

We'd been in this same position the night before last, but the desperation this time was to feel him inside me, moving against me in the easy rhythm of pleasure. I pulled him down to me. "I want you. Now."

From there, it was just a wild scramble to get out of our clothes then the worship of his hands and mouth on my body. Every kiss, every caress and squeeze and moan, sent me higher.

With a snarl of frustration, I pushed up and rolled him.

He had a moment to look at me, the candlelight illuminating surprised delight, before I kissed him like I was trying to drain him, reached down between us, and guided him into me.

"Fuck, Lya," he groaned against my lips.

And I did fuck him, leaning forward so I could keep kissing him while slowly swiveling my hips so he'd hit all the right spots. He helped, grasping my hips and pushing up as though he couldn't possibly get deep enough inside me to satisfy either of us.

The air filled with the scents of ash and herbs as we chased completion with each other.

Iunt

Finally it hit me, so hard and intense that I bowed over him and sank my teeth into the meat of his shoulder as I clenched around him. He threaded his fingers through my hair and held me there, even as I bit hard enough to taste blood. Then he came with a gasping growl as he buried his face against my neck but not his teeth.

We stayed like that, panting, until I was able to gather myself enough to slip free and topple to the side.

Cade gathered me close, pressed his forehead to mine in the dark, with one hand on my hip. "As much as this scares me... I'm yours, Lya. Even if you never let me drink from you again. I'm yours. For as long as you'll have me."

"That might be a while," I whispered back. My heart pounded at what we were offering each other, however obliquely.

"Then it's a good thing I have an eternity."

I didn't, but I'd happily stay with him for every moment I did have. After so long bitterly resenting the fact that nobody had loved me enough to speak up for or claim me, here I had someone who'd done more than that.

He'd fought beside me. Fought *for* me. Battled his sire and his instincts, gone into a second exile with me rather than take advantage of or dump me and continue on his way.

"I love you," I whispered, glad the candlelight was low enough he couldn't see me flush as the admission leaped from a tongue loosened by pleasure and exhaustion.

"Good. Because I love you too, and it'd take more than a stake to stop my heart beating for you." He pulled me closer, and I burrowed into his chest to take in the granite smell of him under the smoky vampire scent, surrendering to the feeling of being safe and adored.

I had no idea what tomorrow would bring, but tonight it brought forever in the arms of someone who'd do anything for me. If there were any more assholes like Morris in Cade's past, they'd get exactly what I dealt out to the first one.

Until then, I planned to enjoy the hell out of life in exile with the vampire who'd stolen my heart.

Want more?

This is the first book in a spin-off series, and there's plenty more to the world of Otherside.

You can get more Shadows of Otherside content in a few different ways:
- Read the original series
  - On Amazon: whwrites.com/soo-series
  - Elsewhere: whwrites.com/books
- Subscribe to Whitney's Patreon for bonus chapters from multiple points of view: whwrites.com/patreon
- Join Whitney on social media:
  - Twitter: twitter.com/write_wherever
  - Instagram: instagram.com/write_wherever
  - Facebook: facebook.com/WhitneyHillWrites

Sign up to the Write Wherever newsletter for updates: whwrites.com/newsletter.

Lastly, if you enjoyed this book, **please consider posting a review**, recommending it on Goodreads or BookBub, or telling a friend who might also enjoy it. As always, thank you for reading, and for your support!

Acknowledgments

If you followed me from the main Shadows of Otherside series, thank you for trusting me to expand the Otherside universe through the eyes of new characters. And if you're joining this world for the first time with this book, welcome! I hope you enjoy your stay.

As always, big thanks go to my family for their incredible support during the writing and publishing process.

My editor, Jeni Chappelle, was amazing (as always) not only in the editing process, but also in helping me with this slight genre pivot. Having that kind of professional guidance as an indie author is invaluable.

To my Shadows of Otherside ARC readers, y'all are everything an author could hope for as book community members! Thank you for sending me your reactions and thoughts. They give me life.

And a last thank you to all the book community at large. To the book bloggers and Bookstagrammers who have helped my books find their audience, thank you for supporting an indie. To local indie bookstores Flyleaf Books and Golden Fig Books, thank you for creating opportunities for indie authors like me in the community. To all of you who read and review, thank you.

I'm so glad to continue this writing journey with you all!

Also by Whitney Hill

The Shadows of Otherside series

Elemental
Eldritch Sparks
Ethereal Secrets
Ebon Rebellion
Eternal Huntress

The Otherside Heat series

Secrets and Truths

The Flesh and Blood series (as Remy Harmon)

Bluebloods

About the Author

 Whitney Hill is an author and speaker. The bestselling first book in her Shadows of Otherside series, *Elemental*, was the grand prize winner of the 8th Annual Writer's Digest Self-Published E-Book Awards and a Finalist in the Next Generation Indie Book Awards.

When she's not writing, Whitney enjoys hiking in North Carolina's beautiful state parks and playing video games.

Learn more or get in touch: whitneyhillwrites.com
More books by Whitney: whitneyhillwrites.com/original-fiction
Sign up to receive email updates: whwrites.com/newsletter

Join her on social media:
- Twitter: twitter.com/write_wherever
- Instagram: instagram.com/write_wherever
- Facebook: facebook.com/WhitneyHillWrites

Get bonus content on Patreon: patreon.com/writewherever

CPSIA information can be obtained
at www.ICGtesting.com
Printed in the USA
LVHW011139230322
714108LV00015B/1073

JUL 2 6 2022